Murdio

GUILLERMO F. PORRO III

©2017

CHAPTER ONE
First Strike

BETWEEN THE WARM SKIES and holy ground of Zithon sits a single structure. Sunshine cascades across its walls, even as it stands high on the Plains of Peace. All around, guards pace in their golden armor, watching for any sign of danger. Inside, the Heavenly Father sits with His feet on a floor of galaxies.

Suddenly from out of the blue skies, two shadows appear. They begin to grow, catching the attention of the guards, who watch as the shadows grow larger until they make their landing. Before them, the figures stand still even as their wings droop down their backs. One by one the guards begin to surround the motionless beings. On their approach, their eyes fixate upon the new additions as they drop to a kneel.

"What is your business with the Father?" asks one of the guards. The two keep their heads down, while the guards place a hand on their weapons at their silent response, bristling at the thought of attack.

"We have news of demonic presence," replies one of the angels before lifting his face to the others.

The swarm of guards steps back in shock at the sight of his face. Half of the angel's face is stripped of skin, revealing his bloodied skull underneath. His eye is intact, while his muscles pulse and thread throughout.

"You must show the Father now," says the guard. They continue to back away allowing them the space to rise back to their feet. The two angels scurry inside underneath the massive archway, following the guards, who glance briefly over their shoulders before returning to their posts along the walls.

The two angels walk quickly into God's chamber, feeling frightened before Him. Keeping his face turned away from God's sight, the angel takes his first step upon the floor; the very floor where the Father can create the heavens and take in the beauty of His work. With each step, a footprint forms upon the surface.

God, sensing their presence, turns around and watches them stop before him. They drop to their knees, their faces angled toward the floor. "What news have you brought me?" God rumbles before placing his hands upon their shoulders.

One of the angels looks up and turns to the other who keeps his face down. "Show our Heavenly Father the damage," he whispers.

God turns His head to the other, taking His hand off his shoulder. After a moment, the angel lifts his head, allowing God only a momentary glimpse before placing his hands upon his face in shame.

"There is no need for shame between these Holy Walls," says God, putting His hand on the angel's other shoulder. The angel slides his hands down past his eyes, seeing the calming look of God's sight before him. He then lowers his hands to reveal the damage done to his face.

Surprise crosses God's face as He looks at the angel, taking in the injury. His hands fall limply to His sides, while the shame creases the angel's face once more. He turns his eyes away as God shakes His head slowly, His white hair swaying gently around His shoulders.

"Father, can this be undone?" asks the angel in desperation.

Without an answer, God lifts His hand and places it upon the angel's boney forehead. First, a blinding light fills the room and shoots out the archway. Next, the angel watches as God slowly moves His hand down to his eye, which he shuts in anticipation. Making its way downward, a shining light fills God's hand, which He continues to move toward the bottom of the angel's jaw. Once God's hand slides off the point of the angel's chin, God steps back.

The angel reaches up to feel his face. "Did it work?" he asks.

"Let me show you," replies God, smiling gently at them.

He then makes his way to the side of the room to grab hold of a golden staff. God points the staff at the floor, a light beginning to leach into the ground in front of it. The light clears all images from the floor and creates a reflection of the angel, much like a mirror. The angel cautiously removes his hands to look down at his image. His eyes widen as he sees his reflection.

Completely normal, without a scar, the angel places his hands on his face. Despite his disbelief, the angel grins and looks to his partner, who nods approvingly.

God lowers His staff, drawing their eyes to Him. "What evil causes such a corruption of one's body?" asks God.

"The darkness of the Fallen, Holy Father," replies one of the angels before bowing his head.

"Please stand, Valren and Jusic," commands God. "Tell me what happened."

They rise to their feet, standing just short of God's eye level. Valren glances once more down at his complexion before the floor returns to its original state of swirling images of stars and galaxies, moons and planets.

"We were doing patrols there when we were attacked," replies Jusic before looking over at Valren. He points to one of the images shifting in God's direction.

God turns to it and, with a flick of the staff, the image grows larger before their eyes. It then lifts upward, rising from the floor between the three of them. God then places His hand beneath it and, with a flick of His wrist, spins the object, getting a full view.

"Serpeda," says God before the image can make a complete rotation.

"What shall we do?" asks Valren.

Valren and Jusic watch God snap His fingers, causing the image to explode into particles. Their eyes follow the dissipating particles, watching as the picture reappears beneath their feet. Once in view, it maneuvers itself into orbit among the others in the floor.

"First, you must find my greatest warrior among the angels," replies God. He watches as Jusic and Valren look to each other in confusion.

"Who would that be?" Valren asks, turning back to God.

"Murdio," thunders God.

"Where shall we find him?" asks Jusic.

"Inside of his aura, on top of the Cumulo," replies God, pointing toward one of the windows.

In the distance, a massive yellow sphere sits just beyond the realm of the kingdom, perched atop a platform of swirling, towering clouds. The two angels look back at God, who nods for them to go there.

As they start to make their way towards it, God looks at them, walking in sync. "One last thing," says God, causing them to stop in their tracks.

The two turn around, standing on the edge of the floor of universes. They watch as God takes several steps, stopping in front of Jusic.

"Yes, Holy Father? Is there anything else?" asks Jusic. He watches in confusion as God step toward Valren.

Just as awkward silence falls around them, God suddenly moves one of his hands back and then charges it forward. It pierces Valren's golden armor and emerges from between the angel's wings, eliciting a gasp from the startled angel. Jusic looks on in shock at Valren, who looks down at God's arm.

Valren's eyes follow God's arm upwards to His body before looking up at his face. Valren's blue eyes suddenly begin to lose all color, allowing darkness to claw its way inside. A smirk suddenly creeps onto his face as he clasps both of his hands onto God's arms. A mighty scream tears from his lips as Valren attempts to yank God's arm from his body.

God's eyes sparkle with white light, His hand beginning to glow as it protrudes from the demonic being. The light starts to swell into the demon's body as Jusic looks on in horror.

Before he can do anything to stop it, Valren's body begins to melt onto the stony ground. The demon turns his gaze to Jusic, as if to plead for help, before Valren completely liquefies into a puddle on the ground.

God shakes the demon's goo from His hand as he looks over at Jusic, whose eyes have begun to fill with darkness once again. As his eyes turn completely black, his features start to change. His teeth sharpen his darkening skin, hiding the draping black feathers appearing from his back. "You are going to pay for that," roars the demon before twisting his head.

It jumps upwards, taking a mighty swing at God.

With ease, God blocks the demon's claws with His staff, flinging the monster to the floor. Once again, He steps toward the monster and unleashes an earth-shattering punch into the demon's core.

The demon briefly grimaces before its smirk returns as God's hand appears out of its back. This time, however, God watches as the demonic power begins to wrap around his hand, the skin growing as if to consume Him.

"Not this time," the demon screams.

Without an answer, God pulls His arm back to allow his hand to sink inside. In His opposite hand, God summons a halo, which he shoves inside the demon's chest. Shining light begins to radiate from out of the demon's body.

The demon screams in agony, the glow erupting from his mouth. Unable to break free, the demon looks down at its glowing body as God rips out His hands.

God then steps back, watching the darkness drip from the demon's eyes like disgusting tears. The monster begins to convulse, the light growing and spreading until finally, the light fills up its entire body.

"I shall grant you mercy," replies God. "An end to your suffering."

The beast's body suddenly explodes with light. The blinding light fills the room escaping from the various openings throughout the chamber. After a moment or two, the last of the light fades revealing only God. Seeing everything without flaw, God finds only a tiny puddle of demonic material still on the floor.

"Chalima, I require your assistance!" God yells.

His voice echoes through the empty room, the sound of footsteps meeting His ears. An angel charges in, her flowing auburn hair revealing the radiant pearl skin on her face. On her approach, her true height reveals itself along with a set of dark brown eyes which examine the room. Coming closer, Murdio watches the white feather making up her wings gently graze the ground. Upon her arrival, she kneels on the edge of the stone, revealing the silvery halo among the bronze armor plating over her chest.

"Yes, Father?" Chalima asks patiently.

"Visit Murdio and send in Matiek to clean up this," God orders.

He points to the puddle, Chalima's eyes following His finger. Her jaw drops at the sight of the demonic material, but she snaps it closed quickly, looking back to God. Without words, she bows her head and runs outside. Before the silence can settle, another round of footsteps can be heard. Another angel with his short hairs swaying with each step runs into the chamber. A scar running from his hazel eye toward his stern jawline which remains in place on his approach. Even despite his short stature combining with the weight of the armor, his steps remain fluent and brisk. With one final step, the angel comes to a stop allowing his breath to normalize.

"How may I be of service?" asks Matiek breathlessly, kneeling before Him.

God waves his hand, allowing Matiek to rise to his feet.

"I need you to—" God stops suddenly, tilting His head. The floor is bare and clean, not a drop of demonic essence present when Matiek turns to follow God's gaze.

"What is it?" asks Matiek, glancing between God and the floor in confusion.

"Never mind, just go back to your post until I summon you," God commands. Continuing to stare in confusion, God places his fingers on his forehead with his thumb near his right temple before sliding it upward. Lifting it up only after reach thing back to His head.

Matiek bows before turning to the open doorway. Alone, God walks toward the window, watching a cloud rise above the kingdom. His staff makes a soft sound against the floor, which echoes throughout the chamber. Chalima soon appears by His side.

She bows her head before turning to face the cloud. Her eyes follow it upwards, finding the white lining at the very top. Lightning begins to chain through the inside of the cloud, thunder echoing inside the chamber. Channeling downward, a bolt of lightning suddenly launches downward, landing just beyond the edge of the kingdom with a massive explosion of light and heat.

Chalima spreads her feathery wings, turning her attention toward the sky. With a single flap, she launches into the air. She spirals upward with the cloud, coming closer to the top. Her eyes are fixed on the slowly expanding cloud, the blue sky stretching higher and higher. Finally, she reaches the top of the towering cloud, seeing a flat top hovering above the kingdom. A glowing sphere of yellow light sits atop the cloudy platform, a figure inside, legs crossed.

Chalima gently floats above the cloud, easing down onto the surface. Feeling the firmness beneath her feet, she lowers her wings to her sides. She stares in wonder at the brightness of the field. She steps closer, surprise filling her when the ground shakes, sending waves over the cloud's surface like ripples. Before her eyes, the ripples sink beneath the cloud, becoming intense bolts of lightning. As thunder echoes around her, Chalima looks over at the wall of yellow light.

She steps closer to the wall, realizing it had become cloudier as she came closer. Only a step away, Chalima turns her head, admiring the wall's ability to obscure the figure. Her eyes strain as she tries to see beyond the wall. After a moment, the color begins to fade, allowing her to better see the man inside. His youthful skin glows from the bright light all around.

"Murdio is that you?" Chalima yells.

The man inside doesn't flinch at the sound of her voice.

"MURDIO!" Chalima yells once again.

Again, the man remains with his hands on his lap. Finally, in anger, Chalima slams her fist into the wall, causing it to ripple with the force of her blow. Suddenly, the wall cracks from the epicenter all the way around. She watches as the being's eyes open to reveal their true color. The roof of the aura begins to fold downwards in sections, causing Chalima to step back.

"Who disturbs my aura?" a voice roars out.

The aura continues to fold down, causing the light to disappear quickly. As it reaches the last piece, it rapidly falls beneath the cloud's surface allowing Chalima inside. With caution, Chalima steps toward him, keeping her eyes on Murdio. Standing straight up, Chalima watches Murdio's wings drape over his shoulder even as his gaze remains to the cloud beneath them. The brief flashes of light all around causing his shadow to darken the space between them. Getting closer, Chalima discovers more as she stands feet from someone equally as tall. In silence, she watches his head lift up, sending her kneeling at his feet.

Chalima lowers her head. "My name is—"

"Chalima, I know," Murdio interrupts.

"Then why ask who I was?" Chalima asks in frustration, rising to her feet.

"When I am channeling, sometimes I lose sight of features," Murdio replies simply. Once more, Murdio's eyes shut before reopening to allow Chalima to watch as the icy blue color returns to his eyes With his vision clear, Murdio looks over at Chalima seeing her golden armor. "So why has a guard of the Holy Father come to see me?"

Chalima looks over her shoulder at God's Kingdom before looking back over at Murdio. "Your Father requires your services," Chalima says, motioning down to the kingdom.

Murdio silently makes his way past Chalima. Tall and confident, he stands on the edge of the clouds, leaving footprints in his wake. Murdio lifts his wings, looking up at the halo over his head. It starts to glow brightly as Murdio turns his eyes toward the sky. "Let's go," he says.

Chalima watches in surprise as Murdio dives off the cloud with his wings tucking into his sides. She runs to the edge to watch his descent, following after him. The air pushes down on them, allowing them to fall faster before Murdio opens his wings to glide. He directs himself toward his Father's chambers, Chalima doing the same.

Her iridescent feathers spread outward, allowing her to catch the air, following in Murdio's wake. She watches him circle, continuing to get closer to the ground. "After me, sir," Chalima says before peeling back her wings to gain more speed.

Murdio watches her pass him, her wings expanding completely, slowing her speed on the approach. Unleashing one final flap of his wings, the force shoots him just behind her. Landing easily, Chalima tucks her wings against her back. After a couple steps, Murdio plants himself beside her, tucking his wings behind as well.

"That was some aerial expertise," Murdio jokes, causing Chalima to pause.

Chalima offers a small smile, turning her eyes toward two guards approaching them. Murdio suddenly smirks before stepping in front of Chalima.

"What are you doing?" Chalima asks in confusion.

"Just greeting some of the guards," Murdio replies, humor in his voice.

Murdio continues forward as the two guards attempt to block his path. He takes another step closer, causing them to reach down for their weapons. Ignoring the threat, Murdio moves forward again, forcing the guards to draw their weapons. Before another step can be taken, Chalima jumps between them.

"What are you doing?" she demands. "Put your weapons away this instant."

The guards look at her, surprise on their faces. "Chalima, welcome back," one guard says as they lower their weapons. Murdio exhales, watching Chalima scowl at the two angels.

"Thank you," she says tersely. "I am bringing Murdio to see the Heavenly Father."

"Murdio? As in the great warrior?" the guard asks, looking appalled at his own behavior.

"From the very top of the Thunderhead," Chalima replies smugly.

Murdio nods his head in greeting.

"Pardon our intrusion, Chalima, we have had imposters intrude upon these halls," the guard says hastily, both of them bowing to Murdio.

"No need for apologies," Murdio says easily. "I understand the power my aura can release." Murdio grins at the dumbfounded look on their faces.

Chalima sighs at the sly smile on Murdio's face. She knows he was just testing them, but it wasn't exactly nice.

"Murdio, my son, please come inside," a voice calls from within the dark doorway beyond the stairs. The guard moves away, allowing Murdio to answer his Father's call.

Once inside, they make their way to God's chamber. God turns from the darkening sky outside to see them standing in the doorway.

"Does my Father require my service?" Murdio asks, kneeling upon the ground.

God nods, beckoning Murdio forward onto the universal floor. With each step, a glowing footprint appears, causing Chalima to hesitantly step forward. After taking a breath, she makes her way closer with her eyes downward. Hypnotizing as it is, she looks up to see God staring at her.

"Please leave us Chalima," God says.

Chalima bows before taking off allowing God to return his attention to Murdio.

"I need you for a mission," God says, turning his attention to the swirling worlds beneath their feet.

Murdio looks down to see each image disappear, a single dot emerging. Together they watch it grow larger. As it approaches their feet, it stops, sending a wave of darkness through the floor. A single black ring wraps around it, while lightning entangles the surface.

"What is that?" asks Murdio, kneeling to get closer. He places his hand firmly on the ground, silent as God kneels beside him.

"A Fallen Colony," God replies.

Murdio removes his hand as God places His in its place, except God goes through and pulls out the image. God then stares at the enlarging image as the masses on the surface intensify, revealing even the tiniest mountain chain.

"I thought we took care of them," Murdio says unhappily.

"Apparently not," God replies.

Murdio looks on as the image continues to spin just above God's hand. "What do you need me to do?" Murdio asks.

"Take a group of angels and defeat any fallen residue," God replies. Before Murdio answers, God reaches down with His other hand and expands the image. It enlarges and reveals the surface under the dark skies. Hidden by a soulless fog, an ancient mausoleum sits on a ground of dirt and ash. Its only sources of illumination are the flashing lightning and dimly-lit, worn torches.

"When?" Murdio asks.

God lifts His hand, summoning three guards inside as He pushes the planet back into the ground. The image sinks below, making its way back into position.

Satisfied, God looks back at the three angels and Murdio. "You must go now," God commands. "But first, I have something for you."

Murdio watches God make His way to the window, grabbing His staff from the where it hovered off the ground. He slowly makes His way back to Murdio, holding the staff before Him. Before Murdio can speak, the staff's golden exterior begins to melt. Fat golden drops slide downward, growing into a puddle at their feet.

Murdio watches on in confusion, surprised when God points at the puddle. Murdio watches as it begins to swirl, the pool rising and spinning inward, causing it to take a new shape. Suddenly, an intense light explodes from the liquid, forcing the group to shield their eyes. It quickly fades, however, allowing them to see the new form in the air. Before them, a shining sword with a gold handle remains. Murdio's eyes widen when he begins to make his way closer.

"Is this for me?" Murdio asks, his eyes drinking in the sword.

"It is, my son," God replies, looking down at staff to His side.

Murdio pauses, studying the sword. He makes his way around it, taking in all its features. Its blade glittering in the sunlight, curves away from his sight even as it locks itself within a metallic hilt. A large M breaks up the golden handle with its ruby red design.

His back to God, Murdio tilts his hand to grasp the handle. Continuing to look down at it, the featherweight blade slices through the air with every motion of Murdio's hand.

Murdio looks down in surprise when it snaps to his side, a sheath and belt forming around the blade and wrapping around his hips. He then takes a couple of steps towards the others who remain silent in awe. Murdio turns to face God.

"With my new weapon, I am ready," he says.

God nods, leaning against His staff. "What will you name your new weapon?" God asks. "Such a fine blade deserves a name."

Murdio looks down at the sword at his side, thinking for a moment. He smiles slightly as he looks up at God. "The Blade of Murdio," he says.

God seems pleased with his choice, and He nods His head once more. "With a worthy weapon at your side, go dispatch of some Fallen."

"In Your name," Murdio says proudly. He bows to God, the soldiers behind him doing the same.

After God taps the staff on the ground, Murdio and his group straighten.

"Farewell, my Choir, may you bring forth a harmony of vengeance," God says.

Murdio leads the way out of God's chambers, the other angels at his heels. As they reach the open air, they take flight, swooping down into a field. As they land, Murdio turns to face them.

"Before we go any further, tell me your names," Murdio says. The first of three steps forward, turning to Murdio with his green eyes staring heavily. His hand steady to his side, providing a self- confidence unlike the others. A single scimitar between his cloth vest and the buckle of his pants.

"My name is Stanira, and I am the second in command in this fellowship," Stanira replies. He then returns to formation when the next angel of a darker complexion steps forward with his eyes darting around the cloudy environment. His hands with a layer of battle scars twitch softly above the bluish handles of the swords at his sides. His hair stiffens in the faint wind, allowing Murdio to catch a glimpse of a scar from his upper brow down to his left ear.

"The name is Orix," Orix says in a soft voice before stepping back next to Stanira.

Murdio shifts his attention to the final angel who is the tallest of them all. His head towering over the others, turn his head when suddenly he reaches back, bringing forth a shining axe from between his wings. He then slams the end down onto the ground using it as a post, flexing his arms as his hand grasp hold of the blade. His silken robe falls just short of his sandals which wrap themselves around his ankles.

"I'm Chester," Chester growls, gripping his fingers tightly around the axe. A single bead of sweat slides from the short hair on top of his head down the side of his face.

Murdio slowly moves his eyes to make contact with all three before shifting his attention to him.

"How do we plan to get to where we are going?" Orix asks from among the group.

Murdio turns his attention, staring at Orix and then without a word, points to a towering wall of clouds where a stern-looking angel stands guard. The guard carries no weapon, just a pair of silver gauntlets which extend to his elbow. Which even as the group approaches, he remains calm as his brown hair droops down the sides of his face, keeping his hazel eyes free from any hindrance. Coming closer, the group makes out a single cloud medallion within the metal of his chest plate. The color of which blends with the pigment of his skin. Before any word can be spoke, they watch as a single lightning bolt webs its way through the cloud wall.

"The Cloud Gateway," Murdio says.

He leads his team toward the gateway, the angel saluting when he spots them. "Where is the mighty Murdio heading?" the angel asks.

"A colony on the other side of the galaxy," Murdio replies. "The planet of Serpeda."

The angel nods and turns around, reaching into one of the clouds. He pulls out a glowing halo, which he shatters, throwing the golden dust into the gateway. A bright light suddenly begins to zig-zag from above his head down to his feet. Once it reaches his toes, the angel grasps either side, yanking on it apart. The two sides spread wide, revealing a dark image behind the bright exterior. The world which the group just saw inside God's hand begins to take shape.

Around the world, space darker than anything they've ever seen swirls ominously. A ring, massive and rough, containing debris from the planet's formation, barrels around the outside.

Murdio can sense his team's fear. "Are you ready?" he asks, glancing over his shoulder.

The three angels nod before stepping between Murdio and the open gateway. Just before their wings extend, dark tentacles spear through the portal (gateway?) and wrap around their bodies. Before they can scream, it pulls them into the portal. Murdio charges forward before turning to the angel frozen in fear.

"You there, what is your name?" Murdio demands. The sound of his voice breaks the angel's paralyzing fear.

"Matiek, Sir Murdio," he manages, his voice trembling as he glances at the gateway.

They both jump back when dark energy begins to leak from out of the portal and onto the floor. The portal ripples with waves of energy, threatening to collapse.

"Close this up behind me and wait for my signal," Murdio commands, charging forward into the darkness. His wings extend as he launches himself after his comrades.

Once he was out of sight, Matiek steps into the darkness slamming the gateway shut. After it is done, Matiek watches the remaining evil as it sinks beneath the ground. "Be safe, my holy brother," Matiek whispers.

CHAPTER TWO
Rescue and Return

THE PITCH-BLACK GROUND appears underneath a sky of shadows rolling with bolts of lightning. A mausoleum, stands alone in the otherwise barren land, lit up by splintering torches. From out of the emptiness, a beam of light drops down, casting an aura around it.

Murdio lands heavily upon the sandy ground, dust stirring around him as he tucks his wings to his back as the light disappears. He lowers a hand to the ground, feeling grains and slime against his fingers. He jumps when a scream suddenly rings out.

He turns toward the mausoleum, jumping to his feet and running toward the doorway. A broken door hangs limp from rotting hinges, leading into the main room. Hallways gape open on every side. Murdio looks around, seeing broken ceiling beams above him.

"Where are you?" Murdio whispers, continuing to look for any sign of movement.

Before he can investigate further, a shadow suddenly appears down one of the hallways. The sounds of heavy breathing and quick foot-steps begin to echo into the room. Murdio watches as the shadow splits into three, his hand moving toward his sword. The shadows struggle in-side the lit room, revealing his team, wounds covering them from a battle against a demon. Their faces are pained as they approach Murdio, blood, and skeleplasm dripping from their twisted forms. Their grotesque forms are barely held together by their armor as they tremble before Murdio.

"Help—us—" Orix gurgles.

Murdio stares at them in disbelief, trying to think of how to help them, when the torches suddenly extinguish in the room. He draws his sword, stepping in front of them to shield them from further harm as darkness creeps inside. Behind a deafening roar, a human-like creature steps into the chamber, its dark eyes targeting the group. Swirling darkness allows Murdio to hear nothing but his troop's ragged and gurgling breathing.

"What is that?" Murdio whispers, clenching the hilt of his sword tighter.

"The thing—that brou—ght us here," Chester rasps.

Unleashing another roar, the creature lifts its arm-like limbs, which begin to melt into tentacles. It looks down at Murdio as he moves into an attack stance. With a summoning call, shadows begin to fill the open hallways, demonic fiends crawling to surround the angels. Dragging themselves closer, the guards huddle behind Murdio, attempting to draw their bloody weapons.

A demon suddenly lunges and charges towards Murdio. Murdio dodges the strike, swinging his blade with confidence, piercing the demon's skin. His sword slides through the demon with little resistance, the demon falling to the ground, Murdio's blade shimmering like new. Murdio watches as the injured demon struggled on the ground. Preparing for another strike, Murdio grits his teeth as it falls back, suddenly breaking into particles which rise into the air, swirling toward the tentacle-monster.

As the monster absorbs the last of the demon, it steps forward, its tentacles forming back into human limbs. It then looks to the left and right at the scores of demons surrounding Murdio and his companions. It drops its arms and growls threateningly, sending the demons back from them. Reluctantly, they disappear into the stone walls around the room.

As the last one vanishes, Murdio faces the beast before them. His heart drops as the lights around them disappear, covering them in a veil of darkness. Blind, the group presses together, feeling as if the shadows are creeping closer. Silence starts to suffocate the room as they struggle to see, steps echoing around them. Orix suddenly panics, swinging his sword as pain shoots up his leg.

His sword meets steel, clanging filling the darkness. "Why did you hit me?" Chester asks, fright in his voice.

"I felt something," Orix replies, fear and desperation in his voice.

Pin-pricks of light suddenly begin to appear in the sky. The angels turn their eyes upward, gasping as the walls of the mausoleum begin to fall away. The ground quakes as the group struggles to keep their composure. Skeleton trees begin to appear on the horizon, surrounding them in the dead and decrepit forest.

"Something's not right, Stanira," Murdio says.

"What do you mean?" Stanira whispers.

"There is no wind, yet the branches bend," Murdio whispers, feeling the hot, stagnant air around them.

The branches continue to bend with ease until suddenly the air crackles, lightning bolts striking the canopies of the trees. Flames erupt from the cracking bark, sending debris and swirls of smoke into the darkness. As embers fall to the ground, catching the dead wood on fire, long shadows begin to appear around them. Murdio and his crew step back as the shadows begin to swirl, forming a black whirlpool. A grotesque figure begins to emerge, lifting strands of hair to reveal bare skin where a face should be.

"You have come!" the demon bellows.

Murdio lifts his sword, preparing to fight. To his surprise, the flames around them begin to extinguish, leaving them in murky darkness once more. The screams of his companions fill the void around them. Murdio looks back in surprise, finding himself alone with only Stanira by his side. His eyes catch the gentle sway of white feathers as they drift to the ground.

"What is it you want?" Murdio demands angrily, brandishing his blade.

The demon laughs, the sound shaking them to their core with a demonic rumble. Another, lesser demon appears before them, and Murdio readies his weapon, causing Stanira to lift his. Before Murdio can stop him, Stanira charges the monster.

"In the name of the Father!" Stanira screams, raising his weapon over his head.

"Stanira, wait!" Murdio yells, reaching as if to stop his comrade.

The no-face demon sees Murdio's distraction and seizes its chance. It lifts out a crystal dagger from its dark frame, aiming it at Murdio. Before Murdio can turn around, it rams the dagger between the wings on Murdio's back. The blade sinks through Murdio's holy armor, piercing his skin, drawing a cry from his mouth. At the sound, Stanira stops, turning to see Murdio on his knees. The no-face demon remains tall over Murdio as he struggles against the pain.

"MURDIO, NO!" Stanira yells desperately.

Murdio snarls weakly, causing the demon to dig the blade deeper. A burning sensation begins to fill Murdio's body, the blade glowing underneath his skin. His armor starts to melt away, revealing corrupting skin beneath. Dead, black skin sloughs to the ground, baring Murdio's bones, which are becoming infected with the darkness.

Despite the pain, Murdio roars in anger. He spins around, unleashing a deadly strike to the demon. The movement rips a chunk of flesh from his body, sending another round of pain through him. Despite the agony, his sword makes an impact, slicing into the no-face demon's body. Murdio's sword cuts cleanly into its side, causing it to drop the dagger onto the ground and vanish from the sight.

The no-face demon roars in horror, looking down at where the sword has cleaved its side. Blood gushing, the demon begins to fade into the darkness, snarling at Murdio. The Blade of Murdio slips to the ground, Fallen blood staining the blade.

Stanira runs to Murdio, lifting his arm over his shoulder. Knees buckling, Murdio struggles to stay on his feet. Stanira watches in horror as the no-face demon's energy pulses through Murdio, making him weaker and paler with each passing second.

"We need to get out of here," Stanira says, panic in his voice. He clutches Murdio's arm tighter around his neck, preparing for a fight as the trees begin to vanish, the ground rumbling once more.

"Matiek! Get us out of here!" Murdio cries, falling to a knee.

The ground beneath their feet quakes as the walls of the mausoleum begin to jut from the barren soil. Stanira watches as Murdio groans, his wings breaking apart and cracking.

Murdio's eyes roll back into his head as the walls surround them. Just as the roof begins to form, hiding the dark sky, a twinkle of light appears. Stanira watches it shoot down to the floor, crashing through the roof, surrounding him and Murdio. The aura begins to lift them off the ground.

A sudden sparkle of light catches Stanira's attention, surprise filling him as he realizes the light is Murdio's sword. It zips across the floor, landing safely in the hilt at Murdio's side, safely back in its owner's possession. Stanira to feels Murdio go limp, the remains of his wings shattering and evaporating in the light. Beneath them, the roof collapses into the room as the light quickly draws them up toward safety. After the last fragments of light disappear, darkness returns to the crumbling ruins.

From out of the shadows, a creature rises from the soil. It watches the angels making their escape, an angry growl leaving its lips. It steps toward the only lit torch in the mausoleum, grasping it and lifting it toward the splintered roof. The faint embers illuminate the monster's face, revealing patches of dead tissue and skin from its forehead to jaw. Not a single hair covers its body, its eyes pitch black. The angels disappear from sight, and it slams the torch down in rage, snuffing the last embers and disappearing into the darkness.

Meanwhile, the beam bursts through the dark sky and past the swirling storms overhead, returning to the sanctuary of God's Kingdom. Stanira keeps hold of the fading Murdio, glancing at Murdio's festering wound. His insides continue to twist and turn with the demonic energy, which grabs at Murdio's bones. His skin continues to rot away, revealing muscle and sinew beneath it. Finally, Stanira and Murdio arrive in Heaven, angels swarming them.

God rushes toward the gathering angels, who part to allow Him through. God gasps softly as He catches sight of Stanira and Murdio's wounds. He reaches for the angels, His eyes fading to white with His power. He lifts His hands, which starts to glow in the pure air, pressing them first against Stanira's face and then against Murdio's back, a loud hiss echoing as they make contact. He moves His hands over their gaping wounds, which begin to repair themselves.

Underneath His touch, the tissue returns to normal, the evil energy inside their bodies starting to retreat. Finally, God releases His power, letting His hands fall to His sides. Both Stanira and Murdio take in slow breaths, realizing their pain is gone.

Stanira bows deeply in gratitude. "Thank you, Father," he says, relief in his voice.

God nods, His eyes still fixed on Murdio's bare back.

Despite no longer being in pain, Murdio still winces as he moves to his feet. He lifts his hand over his shoulder to feel the soft skin. "What happened?" Murdio asks out of confusion. "Where are my wings?" He can feel the loss of his wings, their weight gone, and sadness seeps into him.

"You were ambushed," God says. "Matiek, your guardian angel, came to your rescue. But now your divinity is under attack."

Murdio looked at God in confusion. "My divinity?" he asks softly. "Will my wings grow back?"

God nods slowly. "But only you can bring them back." God motions for Murdio to walk with Him. "We will speak further."

Murdio turns to Matiek then to thank him, when suddenly a crippling pain shoots up his body. He wraps his arms around his chest, dropping to his knees. Demonic energy begins to attack him once more, burrowing into the muscles in his head and rising to the top of his skull. Murdio screams in pain, pressing his hands against the sides of his head. The halo floating over him begins to twist, darkness causing it to crack and threatening to shatter it.

Before it can completely shatter, God charges forward with staff in hand, uttering a powerful command. At the sound of His voice, the darkness dissipates, allowing Murdio's halo to return to full power.

"Am I not healed?" Murdio gasps in subsiding pain.

"Time heals all wounds," God says softly. He looks at the angels surrounding them, motioning His hand. The angels disperse at His command, leaving them alone.

"Even my divinity?" Murdio asks, struggling to draw his sword. His heart sinks at the sudden weight of the blade, and at the demonic fluid that now stains the metal. He looks back to God, laying his sword flat on the ground in front of Him.

"Yes, even that," God says gently. "However, the demonic energy must purge itself from your body."

"How much time do I need?" Murdio asks.

"It is complicated," God answers, a grimace pulling at His face.

"What do you mean, Father?" Murdio asks.

"Your body and your spirit are not complete," God replies.

Murdio frowns in confusion before silently looking himself over. Nothing seems out of the ordinary until he runs his hand in between his ribs. He stops, rubbing what feels like a hole beneath his skin.

"What is that?" Murdio breathes, alarmed as he looks to God.

"The demon that attacked you took a piece of you with him," replies God.

Murdio turns his attention back to the sinking skin. "Can't we just retrieve it?" Murdio asks. He then looks over at Matiek, standing next to the cloud wall.

"Unfortunately, my son, this is like a broken human heart," God says. "It needs time and focus."

Murdio frowns, lowering his head to look at the gleaming sword at his feet. "So what can I do?" he asks.

"Follow me," God says lifting His golden staff. He turns around, making His way toward an opening.

Murdio lifts his heavy sword off the ground and follows God down the path. Walking side by side, they make their way through an area of the kingdom which Murdio has rarely seen. This area of Heaven is known as the Forbidden Divinity, where the angel-soldiers train for battle. It is empty except for God and Murdio, because of the peace that exists in the universe.

Continuing down the winding pathway, they approach a large vault. A massive building sitting in the center, clean and bright, its marble shines from the sunlight, forcing Murdio to blink against the brightness. Once his eyes adjust, Murdio sees a massive slab blocking the doorway.

"Father, what is this place?" Murdio asks, looking over to God.

Without a word, God approaches the vault, placing His hand along the face of the stone. He peels back the rock, revealing the inside of the building. Murdio steps forward, examining it as God steps back. Murdio admires the floor to ceiling pillars in all corners, which hold up a solid piece of marble that makes up the roof, keeping the inside cool.

"This is a resting place for my warriors," God answers.

"Is this where I am to heal?" Murdio asks. God nods his head simply as Murdio looks down at his sword. He looks over his shoulders, taking in the emptiness.

"My son, you need to rest and recover," God says, leaning against his staff. "You need to regain your strength to once more wield your Blade."

Murdio turns around and looks down upon the sword a final time. He then holds it out to God, knowing He will keep it safe while he heals. God reaches out slowly, wrapping His hand around it and lifting it from Murdio's grasp with ease. Murdio bows to God before turning his attention back to the open room. After taking a couple of steps in silence, Murdio stops and drops his head.

"One last thing Father," Murdio says, causing God to pause. "Why did they take my bone?"

God breathes a slow sigh, drawing Murdio's gaze. "You are the strongest warrior and body that has ever been made from my spirit," God whispers. "I believe they hope to make a demonic creature with your attributes and skills."

Murdio looks down at the floor before taking a deep breath. Once inside, he turns around to look at God. "How shall I continue to grow my skill?" he asks.

God's staff begins to glow, the walls suddenly starting to shake. The marble starts to grow and take shape, forming the body of an angel. Once complete, the angel's eyes open and it stands at attention, waiting for two more of its kind.

Murdio watches as the last two drop from the wall, revealing the perfect marble behind them.

"You are going to need this," God says, tossing the golden staff into the room.

Murdio catches it looking down at the large weapon. Approaching from both sides, the marble angels get closer, reaching down to grab hold of maces built from their very bodies. With a smirk, Murdio turns around to look at God.

"Come and get me, Father, when the demons decide to show," Murdio calls. He watches one of the guards hover overhead and fly downward with its mace in hand. He slides away, striking it in the back, knocking chunks of rock from its body.

"I shall so enjoy your fight for a temporary eternity," God says, slowly sliding the slab back into the frame.

From His own viewing place, God watches the battle wage on between Murdio and the stone guards. One of the guards rams Murdio into the wall, causing the building to shake down to the foundation, making God smirk. To prevent any intrusion, God has fused the door into the stone around it, forming one solid piece. The sound of weapons on stone echo daily through God's Kingdom as He watches the fight.

Beside the vault, the Blade of Murdio is sunk into the soil where God tossed it, waiting for the day that its bearer will emerge once again. It carries the weight of God's parting words, "May the Blade of Murdio return to him when he needs it for battle."

CHAPTER THREE
Four Years Later

A S THE YEARS PASS, the Fallen grow in numbers, becoming testier and finding new ways into God's kingdom. Even with the angels' many victories over them, still their numbers swell. And so, the need to protect God did, too. New barriers begin to rise, such as a single golden door between God and his angels, offering sanctuary and another line of defense from the demons.

Inside God's chamber, He made His way around the room, watching the time pass beyond the walls and golden door. A knock as His chamber draws His attention, and He waves His hand to unlock the golden door. He looks up when Matiek enters the room, seeing the look on his face.

"Pardon my intrusion, Father, but I have come to inform you another group of trainees has begun their instructions," Matiek says with a bow.

God looks up as His large throne floats down, made of thundering clouds. It lands gently on the floor, lightning shooting from the back. As God takes His seat, the clouds solidify, electricity flowing throughout.

"That is good, Matiek," God says, looking down at the floor of galaxies. "I feel a darkness growing in the universe. We must be prepared."

The galaxies begin to spin around the chair, a single planet made of darkness emerging. God holds out His hand, summoning it upwards. He sighs as he looks at it, darkness rolling over it, forming a band through the middle of the planet. Matiek flinches at God's anger, watching him toss it away, a pillar forming to catch it.

"The world of the Fallen," God sneers, watching the rotating planet.

"What are you going to do with it?" Matiek asks.

"I will look upon it," God replies. His hands grab hold, His eyes turning white while Matiek watches.

Matiek watches the planet carefully, seeing the darkness continue to rise. "I see no change," he says quietly. He looks outside, seeing the blue sky darken before returning to the light. Countless days fade into night, causing Matiek to lose track.

Years pass as God watches the world grow darker, the band around the middle stretching to engulf the planet. He tightens His grasp sending another surge of His light, hoping to change the outcome.

Matiek sees the darkness come to a crawl near the poles. It waivers slightly against God's power, but ultimately reaches the ends.

God sighs in defeat as He rewinds time, the darkness returning to its former state. The strain in God's hands ease as another knock sounds at the golden door. "Enter," God calls.

A single angel enters the room, bowing before them.

"Yes, Colathus, what is it?" God asks, His hands resting on His legs.

"Forgive me—the others—we couldn't—" Colathus' lips quiver, causing him to stumble over his words. Before long, a group of angels gingerly step inside from the corridor. Trying to catch their breath, they fall to their knees.

"We have failed you, Father," one of the angels gasps.

"No, rather you succeeded," God says in a stern tone. The group look at one another before turning their gaze back to God.

"How so?" Colathus asks, regaining his composure.

"For you see, they have revealed the location of the halo that is unbroken," God replies.

"I don't understand the strength of a single halo," Colathus replies in confusion.

"One halo can deliver divinity onto a spirit of high faith," God replies.

"What is our next move?" Colathus asks, his voice still trembling.

"It is time," God says. "We must restore ultimate balance. There is only one who can deliver the halo without being broken."

"Who is that?" Colathus asks.

God rises from the throne, causing bolts of electricity to bounce around the room. God watches His kingdom, seeing time passing before him. Troops move through, remembering the powerful angelic heroes and trying to listen for any signs of eternal battle. However, only silence comes forth, along with a wave of fog which covers the area.

From out of the mist, a group of shadows begin to form into a troop of training angels following in line behind another angel. The group of trainees follow their commander, making their way through the graveyard towards a vault. As the angels come closer, they step gingerly between debris, keeping their armor and weapons tight to their sides. The commander stops before the vault, turning to his trainees.

"This is the resting place of Murdio, and he remains inside until the Fallen choose to attack our kingdom," he says to his troop.

"Why is he in there?" one of the trainees asks.

"To heal, and to further develop his skills," the commander replies.

The trainees stare in silence at the vault, when suddenly one of the trainees spots a sword handle poking out of the ground.

"Commander, what is that?" the trainee asks, pointing to the sword handle.

The commander looks down at the sword and then back to him. "That is the mighty Blade of Murdio, which awaits him to wield it once more," he says.

As the trainees look on in awe, a sudden darkness begins to encase the place, a chill swirling in the air. The commander's eyes widen as he turns around, seeing a Fallen demon sitting on one of the headstones.

"How dare you disturb this place, cretin!" the commander yells, drawing his sword.

The trainees turn around, brandishing their swords, watching the demon step down from the headstone and begin to walk toward the group. The trainees backed away in fear, closer to Murdio's resting place, having never seen a demon up-close before.

"We must protect Murdio!" the commander yells. "Prepare for battle!"

The trainees lift their weapons and shields, preparing for whatever the demon has for them. The demon pauses before the group, its lavender eyes sparkling as it draws a spear from the shadows of its cloak. It grins evilly at their reaction, stalking toward the edge of the churchyard). With a devilish growl, the demon suddenly launches his spear. The angels dodge it, the spear slamming into the stone of the vault.

"You fool, you lost your aim!" a trainee taunts. Surprise fills him as the demon grins, pointing a rotting finger at the tomb. All of the soldiers turn to see dark tendrils beginning to dig into the stone.

"Pull it out!" the commander yells as he grabs hold of the spear.

One by one, the trainees all grab the spear trying desperately to pull it out with all their strength. Leaving them to deal with the spear, the demon slinks away, escaping.

The angels struggle to remove the spear, watching the evil spread, corrupting Murdio's vault. Finally, they yank the spear away, demon spirits exploding out of the hole. Once the spirits disappear and the chaos calms, the trainees turn to their commander.

"What was that?" one of the trainees asks breathlessly.

"I don't know, but I hope we weren't too late," the Commander says, looking down at his hands. The darkness of the spear has eaten away at his skin, revealing the bones underneath. He looks at his troop, seeing their hands the same shape.

"Can this be healed?" a trainee asks, fear on his face.

The Commander nods his head, closing his eyes. Halos suddenly encase his wrists, repairing the damage done. As the troops watch their hands heal, the ground begins to tremble. They struggle to stay on their feet, the commander turning to the vault to see the door shaking violently.

"Trainees, go now to our Father and inform him of what has transpired!" the commander orders, sending them flying into the air.

As they vanish, the commander watches as a sudden burst of light erupts from the door frame. The massive slab covering the entrance then shatters, causing the commander to raise his arms to shield himself from the rumble as a bright light bursts from the tomb. As the light fades away, the commander drops to his knees, bowing his head.

"Murdio, you've arisen!" a deep voice booms.

The commander turns, seeing the trainees hiding behind God, before he looks up. He is surprised to see a powerful and tall angel towering over him. As if not a day has passed, his blondish hair stands on end above his green eyes. Blood drying upon his knuckles even as he flexes his fingers from off the staff. The staff stiffens, disintegrating on its way to the ground, allowing the particles to float off into the distance. The shadows peeling back, revealing the sparse facial hair all around his face. Before Murdio can speak, the halo above his head darkens, dropping to the floor and shattering on impact. The trainees' jaws drop as the fragments lay on the floor, God standing in silence.

"Father, I'm afraid we are too late," the commander laments, breaking the silence.

God looks down at him. "Commander Daeolus, of what do you speak?"

Daeolus gulps as he stares down at the fragments on the floor. "A Fallen appeared and threw a spear, which corrupted Murdio's vault," he manages.

God shifts his eyes from the halo to Daeolus, whose eyes shut as he shakes in fear. "This is a terrible turn of events," God mumbles as Murdio bends down, silently retrieving the broken fragments.

Murdio stares at them in surprise when the particles suddenly dissipate into the slight wind. "Father ... but I am still Murdio, with or without a halo," he says quickly, desperation in his voice. A single tear slides down his cheek.

"You have been corrupted. I'm sorry," God whispers, His eyes turning away.

Murdio follows his gaze, seeing that his sword has turned into the stone that had built his tomb. "How can I regain the use of my holy weapon?" he breathes, kneeling beside the sword.

"There is only one way," God says slowly.

"What must I do, Father?" Murdio begs. He stands stalwart before God, ready to prove himself. "I will do any number of trials."

Sorrow fills God as He gazes at His mightiest warrior. "Come with me."

Murdio follows God through pearly gates and past the line of souls receiving their wings and halos. Murdio unconsciously reaches back, his wings still missing even after all this time. "I guess this is more serious than we first thought," Murdio mumbles as he follows God.

God nods as a cloud beneath Him rises up and floats away towards His palace. A cloud forms beneath Murdio as well, drifting after God. They float through a gate and toward the Sapphire Walls. They pass through beautiful fields, soon reaching the palace entrance. The large golden door slides away, allowing God and Murdio entry as their clouds disappear. Once inside God's chamber, the golden door seals shut behind them.

"So this is what heaven has become," Murdio whispers as God settles on his throne of clouds.

"Please, come in, child," God says, beckoning Murdio closer.

"Thank you, Father, for allowing me entrance to this sanctum of Heaven," Murdio says as he kneels. God steps forward and places His hand on Murdio's shoulder, allowing Murdio to rise back to his feet.

"Much has changed here since you were sealed away," God says, walking back to His throne, pulling His staff from beside the throne.

"I must find a way to remove this darkness," Murdio says solemnly. "Both within myself and Your Kingdom."

God nods, pointing His staff toward the planet that sits across the room. "This is the Fallen world which has been silent for centuries," God says, sadness filling his eyes. "Until now."

"Why is that?" Murdio asks, walking over to the image.

"The dark spirits have returned to corrupt the souls that wander on this once holy planet," God says softly. His heart aches for His creations.

"Dark spirits?" Murdio asks, confusion in his voice. He watches as an explosion erupts from the planet's surface.

"Yes, my child, and they are trying to increase the size of the Fallen army," God says.

"What does this have to do with me?" Murdio asks, looking to God as He turns to face him.

"They must be stopped," God says passionately. "You have a lot to learn my son, for this has everything to do with you." God regains his composure, walking back to His throne. Murdio follows Him to the throne, watching as He sits down, causing the throne clouds to darken.

"Father, what is my task?" Murdio asks, kneeling once more.

"I cannot tell you, Murdio, instead you must discover it on your own," replies God. "On the surface of the Fallen world."

"Why can't you tell me?" Murdio asks.

"I am unable to intrude on a road to destiny, but I can provide guidance," God says.

Murdio nods his head and looks back at the entrance, a figure suddenly rushing inside. With angels in pursuit, the figure lifts its hand, ripping off the angelic facade, revealing the grotesque face of a Fallen. Murdio's eyes widen as suddenly a spear drops out of the Fallen's robe. As the Fallen raises the spear, it suddenly engulfs itself with darkness, screeching loudly.

Springing into action, Murdio grasps the Fallen's arm and violently tears it from its socket. He drops it onto the floor, watching it dissipate as the Fallen roars in anguish, falling to a heap on the floor. Before it could sink through and escape, God rises from His throne, pointing His staff at the Fallen, trapping it inside the room. He steps back as Murdio places his foot on the Fallen's back, turning to the angels in the doorway.

"How was this scum able to blemish Heaven?" Murdio demands angrily.

"We tried to stop it, but it was too fast," one angel says, dropping his gaze in shame.

"We're sorry Holy Son, but it flew past us," another says breathlessly.

"Oh, and the fact that they can't fly tells me what?" Murdio demands, sensing a lie.

"Colathus, speak now," God commands, turning to him.

"This one did," Colathus says. "It had massive wings made of shadows."

"Murdio, check its back," God orders, pointing to the Fallen on the floor.

Murdio bends down, grasping a fistful of the Fallen's robe, quickly pulling it off. To his surprise, Murdio sees two wings jut from out of the robe as the Fallen lay on the floor. "I see a lot has changed since I was last awake," Murdio says in surprise, watching the wings suddenly shrink and then disappear.

"Indeed Murdio, which is why I need you to go down there," God says sternly.

Murdio looks back at his Father and then at the Fallen on the floor. "Understood," he says. "I must go immediately before something stronger appears." With an easy motion, he crushes the Fallen's head against the floor. He turns and vanishes through the golden door.

God nods His head, looking down at the Fallen on the floor. He shakes His head as He looks up at the angels.

"I'm always cleaning up his mess," says God as He aims His staff down at the body.

It begins to glow, and a cloud below the corpse devours it and returns to its form. God looks up to find he is alone once again, and He turns back to look at the planet. He stares deeply into it, considering Murdio's quest.

Murdio walks into the magical garden that surrounds the building. He stops for a second and looks around at the beauty of the nature blending with the peacefulness of the clouds above. Murdio takes a deep breath and walks back over to the gate of the Sapphire Wall. As he approaches the gate, the angels on the other side watch as he places his hands on the bars of the door, his mind carrying the images of the darkness beyond the gates. Murdio walks to the edge of the kingdom, where an angel carrying a set of wings is awaiting him.

"Father shall be with you in spirit," she says.

"Indeed, He will, and I'm sure I shall spend eternity repaying him," Murdio says, humor in his voice.

The angel shakes her head with a grin, tossing the wings to Murdio, who quickly fuses them to his back. "Remember," she says, "those will fall away when you arrive."

"I remember, Chalima, don't worry," Murdio says.

Chalima nods her head and turns to the wall of clouds next to him. She grasps hold of it and stretches it, revealing a gateway.

Murdio steps forward, standing in front of the swirling air. He looks at Chalima, once again smiling. "Matiek is going to be mad." He stretches the wings out, jumping into the portal as Chalima closes it behind him.

"He is forgiving," Chalima calls after him before her voice quiets to a whisper. "Bless him, Holy Father, for when he arrives he shall be tested greatly."

"I shall bless him once more," God says, His voice filling Chalima's mind. "When he becomes my Holy Son again and takes his rightful place."

CHAPTER FOUR
The Fallen World

THE FALLEN WORLD IS barren, sand and rubble as far as the eye can see. The sky is crimson red with nothing but a black sun breaking the view. A single white cloud appears, and Murdio leaps through, allowing his wings to catch the weak gust swirling around him. He makes his descent, a desolate town in the distance catching his eyes. As he floats down toward it, he sees a sea of red which rushes to meet a barren shore. When his feet hit the dusty ground, the wings drop from his back, fading from sight. Murdio looks around at the dusty terrain that surrounds him in all directions.

He turns to look behind, watching a wave crash along the coastline. Murdio bends down, pressing his fingers into the water, realizing it was thick and sticky. He frowns. "Blood," Murdio breathes.

He looks over at the broken road beside him, a beam of light suddenly shooting out of the sky and crashing into the ground in front of him. Murdio watches as an object drops down to the ground, piercing the dusty sand at his feet. He leans over and grabs the object, his eyes widening as he realizes it is a gold staff. Next to it, a note sits on top of the cracked soil.

"Consider this an assist," Murdio read. He grins to himself, glancing up at the sky.

Murdio strikes the ground with the staff, his skin beginning to turn gray and his robes becoming dirty with the power of the spell. Murdio quickly checks his appearance, feeling a vibration beginning to disturb the sand beneath his feet. Turning his eyes back to the road, he walks toward it, using the staff for aid. When he makes it to the center of the cracked road, Murdio stops, turning to look both ways.

A rumbling down the road can be heard, some sort of machine tossing sand high into the sky. Murdio's eyes turn pure white with a yellowish ring as he focuses his sight in the direction of the sound. He manages to make out a vehicle, leaking a translucent red goo onto the ground.

As the vehicle comes closer, Murdio quickly walks toward the edge of the road, allowing it to pass. As Murdio stares at it, he realizes it is made of skeletons, with some sort of red cement holding it together. Murdio watches in surprise as it comes to a stop in front of him, casting a long shadow over him. Two bloody, skeletal beings appear from out of the top.

"Are you Faithless?" one of the creatures asks in a gurgling voice.

Murdio, staring at the creature, pulls back a sleeve, his skin beginning to fall in chunks to the ground. Stopping at his elbow, all that remains is the bone and dripping blood. "Answer your question?" Murdio asks confidently.

They turn skulled heads to each other, sharing a dark look as they disappear inside the vehicle. A hole opens from the side, between rib bones, allowing them to step out. As their feet touch the ground, the sand swirls, sticking to their bloodied feet. Behind them, the vehicle's muscle panels sew themselves back together and close the hole.

"Why must you hide your strength?" one of the creatures asks. Both watch Murdio's skin heal the open wounds.

"Gives me an edge against God," Murdio says, pulling his sleeve back down.

The creature smirks looking over his shoulder at his gruesome companion. The other makes his way forward. "Very helpful, but don't hide it from allies," the creature says.

Murdio inspects them, eying dark bone daggers on their hips. "Even in the beyond I prefer to go alone," Murdio comments quietly.

"Well then, I'm Spiritist Jazeer, and this is Guard Boziri," says Jazeer as Boziri salutes.

"I am Mozeri," Murdio says.

Jazeer turns to Boziri, a grin on his face. "We apologize for disturbing you, but we are part of the Lost Guard," Jazeer says. "We search for the Undecided."

"Undecided?" Murdio asks.

"You don't know?" Boziri asks, raising his ghastly hand to his chin.

"Sorry, don't get around others much," Murdio lies quickly.

"We force them to either choose our side or suffer a fate worse than death," Jazeer sneers.

"Ah," Murdio says, trying to hide his revulsion.

"Oh well, we shall be off," Jazeer says, turning back to the vehicle. The panel splits, allowing Jazeer and Boziri inside. "There are much more to find."

Murdio stands in silence as the two vanish inside, reappearing in the lookout.

"Farewell," Boziri says with a gargled chuckle as he and Jazeer back out of sight.

The vehicle begins to shake and rumble as they start up the engines. Then, with a psychotic laugh, they roar away, leaving a wake of sand behind it. As Murdio watches it pull away, the goo flows from onto the road before seeping through the cracks within the surface. The vehicle moves out of sight and Murdio turns back in the other direction, unsure of where to go.

"I guess I should follow them," Murdio thinks aloud as he begins walking after it.

Murdio walks for a long time in silence, taking in the landscape. A contrast to Heaven, blood contaminates the ground all around. Hills rise sporadically over the horizon into the crimson sky. A tall building juts out of the sand, breaking the monotony of the sandy hills.

A scream suddenly fills the air, making Murdio jump. He breaks into a run toward the building, realizing it is a house with a collapsing shed to the side of it. He lifts his staff as he comes to the door, ready for danger. He pushes against the door, which crumbles away, revealing an empty room with a set of stairs that have broken halfway up to the second floor.

Murdio pauses inside the door, hearing soft whispers coming from the other side of the wall. Slowly, he pokes his head around the corner, seeing three unclean spirits sitting along the wall at the far end.

"We must keep our heads. Otherwise, we shall be no better than those damn Faithless," one says, causing the others to nod their heads.

"Yes, because soon our God will return to save us," the one next to him says, trying to bring hope into their despair.

Murdio jumps again when they suddenly begin to scream in panic. He turns the corner just as a massive, bloody claw reaches inside, grabbing them and pulling them through the wall. Murdio stares as where they had just been sitting in confusion and disgust.

"What was that all about?" he breathes, looking around the room.

An old trunk on the floor catches his eyes. Murdio slowly walks to it and opens it, finding a cross, some old clothes, and a rusty key. He picks up the old clothes and blew away some of the dust before placing them back inside the trunk. Instead of taking them, he reaches for the cross with one hand and the rusty key with the other. He closes the trunk as he stands, placing the cross inside his robe's inner fold.

Murdio jumps when a crash suddenly echoes through the air. He ran to the window, peeking through the boards that block the sun from inside. When he looks out, he finds two creatures, pacing the land, looking for their next prey.

In their hands they hold large axes that spit darkness. One drops its hood, revealing its skull and empty, frightening eyes. Murdio watches it turn to the empty doorway, pointing toward the house. He holds his staff tightly in his hands, preparing. He hides in the wall's shadow, waiting for them to enter.

The two monsters enter, looking around, noticing the trunk still open. One walks toward it, using its ax to open it wider while the other walks toward the window. The monster turns to the other, motioning him over. As it walks over, looking inside the chest, Murdio steps out, staff in hand. They turn to Murdio, standing halfway in the window's glare.

"Where did you get that?" the creature says, eying Murdio's staff.

"Who cares Dionte, it's ours now," the other says, smiling creepily.

"I was just curious Brax," Dionte mutters, staring at the staff hungrily.

They approach Murdio, hefting their axes.

"Take it then," Murdio says, tossing the staff at them. It hits their skulls, causing them to wail in pain as it burns them. Seizing his chance, Murdio quickly catches his staff, using it to bash Dionte through the wall before turning to Brax.

Brax lifts his axe, anger in his dead eyes. "You'll pay for that!" Brax screams, charging Murdio.

Murdio sprints along the wall, grabbing the trunk and running toward the fireplace. Dionte struggles to get up, staggering back into the room, blood dripping from his eyes. Suddenly, Murdio throws the trunk at them, using his staff to fire a bolt of lightning at the trunk, causing an explosion.

The two monsters crash through the wall, landing in the dust outside. Murdio walks through the hole left behind and looks down at them lying in a pool of shadows. Mild surprise fills him as they move shakily to their feet, blood dripping from their skulls. "Forgot you're already dead," Murdio says, breathing heavily as he readies his staff.

They smirk, walking toward him, axes resting on their shoulders. "So, you're him," Brax says, wiping off his face.

"That means you are looking for it," Dionte says.

"What would I be looking for?" Murdio asks, suspicious.

"The Unbroken Halo," Brax says, turning to Dionte. "Go to the leader and tell him of the dormant one's arrival."

Dionte nods when shadows puddle beneath him, allowing him to disappear.

Anger fills Murdio as Dionte escapes. "May my Father have mercy upon you," Murdio says, preparing an attack.

"He holds no weight here!" Brax yells, charging Murdio. He swings his axe with all his strength, sending it crashing into the wall behind him.

Murdio jumps, bouncing off the axe, landing on the wall using his staff as balance. He turns, dropping behind Brax, preparing for the next attack.

Brax swings once more, his axe lodging into the wall. Struggling to remove it, Brax lets go, pulling a bone from his robe. He twirls it between his fingers, beginning to swipe at Murdio's chest as Murdio retreats inside the house.

Murdio backs up the broken stairs, making his way to the top step as he ducks the creature's attacks.

Brax pulls out another bone, brandishing it with his other hand. He jumps toward Murdio, who grabs his arms and threw him, sending him crashing to the floor. Brax shakes it off, looking up at Murdio standing over him. Brax then rips off his skull, throwing it at Murdio who swings the staff, sending it into the wall. It lands on the ground, Brax's headless body staggering toward the stairs.

Murdio jumps off, and onto the body, piercing the staff into Brax's chest. At the pure contact of Murdio's staff, Brax's head and body begin to turn black, trembling as the darkness attempts to flee. Murdio yanks his staff away and ducks into a room, just as the boney creature explodes, fragments impaling the walls of the house. Murdio looks down at his robe, trying to catch his breath. He sighs as he sees that it is ripped from the battle.

After a moment, Murdio walks over and pulls the clothing that had been in the chest from under the rubble. He rips off his torn robes and pulls on the new clothing, looking to the window as the sound of rumbling fills the air outside. He peeks through the dirty glass, his eyes widening as more creatures step out of their vehicle, axes hanging to their side. He quickly backs away from the window, desperate to find another exit. Finally, his eyes land on a door, which is blocked by a large, up-ended cabinet.

Murdio grabs the top of the cabinet, gritting his teeth as he heaves it away. It lands with a crash, shaking loose plaster from the decrepit walls. Murdio quickly yanks the knob, the sound of footsteps creaking on the floorboards filling the room behind him. A ray of blinding light fills the room as he rushes out, looking for a place to hide.

Murdio spots the doorway to the garage beside the house. He runs to it, shoving the door open and closing it quickly behind him. He tries to catch his breath as he looks through a crack in the wood, seeing the monsters searching the house. He knows he's safe for the moment, and he turns his head, surprise and hope filling him.

A large, dirty tarp is pulled over a lumpy form.

Murdio yanks the sheet away, dust tickling his throat and nose, forcing Murdio to cover his mouth. Brushing cobwebs away, he realizes it's an old motorcycle. Murdio lifts his leg over it and sits on it, realizing it needs a key. He looks around for a moment, but stops, reaching into his pocket.

The key from the trunk!

He places it in the ignition, and, to his surprise, it slides right in. Before starting it, he grabs the staff, lifting it above his head. Light begins to emanate from the staff, covering Murdio and the motorcycle in golden beams. When it fades, Murdio looks down to see that the staff has fused into the motorcycle's metal, turning it a brilliant gold.

"Now this I can use," Murdio says, grinning in admiration.

He finally turns the key, causing it to roar. He throws it into gear, tires spinning as he crashes through the garage door. A blast of light erupts from the muffler, blinding the enemies behind him. Murdio guns it down the road, leaving the creatures in his dust.

For a moment it looks like he will be able to get away, but a thunderous rumbling suddenly catches up with him. He glances over his shoulder, seeing their vehicle hot on his heels. Leaning forward, he presses the throttle harder, his golden motorcycle putting distance between him and the monsters. Just when he thinks he'll escape them, one suddenly explodes.

Two bikes suddenly emerge from the cloud of smoke, the vehicle slamming to a stop. The same monstrous beasts are driving the bikes, trying to keep up with him. The two bikes speed toward Murdio, waves of screams suddenly pelting him.

Losing his balance, Murdio swerves off the road and into the sand. He hits a hill, sending his bike flying into the air. At the peak of his jump, he turns to watch the creatures' bikes stop at the bottom of the hill. Murdio looks forward, his bike landing as he continues to put distance between them. As Murdio hits the cracked pavement again, to his surprise, he rides through a swirling sandstorm and into the city limits.

Taking in the scene, Murdio looks around for any signs of life. However, as he drives past the buildings, nothing stirs. The only sound is the wind breaking the fog of silence. Murdio stops in an intersection when he spots a line of spirits, walking alongside the road. He pulls up to it, watching the spirits move along. In the building nearby, the occasional floater goes through a door, only to reappear seconds later. Curious, Murdio reaches out to touch one, but a hand suddenly grabs him.

"Do not touch!" a blank-faced spirit howls, floating above the ground.

"What are all these spirits doing here?" Murdio asks, pulling his hand away.

"This is limbo," the being says. It waves a ghostly arm. "They must choose their final fate."

Murdio watches one run into the street, dropping to its ghostly knees. It [It would be helpful if you would describe the ghost; man or woman, etc.] looks down as two more spirits appear, each representing a side; the one on the left, a spirit angel carrying a book of the good deeds done by the being, while the other is a skeleton, dripping blood which brings temptation. The ghost looks up at the two, who try to convince it to join. As Murdio watches, the ghost cries out and jumps toward the angel before disappearing with it. The skeleton sneers, turning to where the angel was, before vanishing into a cloud of darkness.

"Sanctuary or Purgatory," Murdio whispers.

"You ask too many questions," the ghost beside him says.

Murdio smirks, watching as the spirit himself undergoes the chosen path.

"Come and join the army of the Holy," the angel says, rising higher into the glowing light. The skeleton smirks, opening his hands, showing him a leader of the Fallen. The ghost looks at both, bones beginning to appear on his frame.

"He has chosen!" the skeleton bellows, the ghost walking toward him. The angel shakes his head, shutting the book, and vanishing. Before the skeleton disappears, he spots Murdio standing behind the ghost. "You've lost another." The skeleton chuckles, its eyes suddenly glowing red as it rushes Murdio.

Murdio jumps from his motorcycle when the gold peeling away and forming a staff in his hands.

The skeleton jumps, surprising Murdio as it passes through him, landing in a pool of shadows.

Murdio looks at the pool, watching as it swirls out of sight, leaving only the cracked and parched earth. He shakes it off, throwing the staff at the motorcycle, turning the bike to gold. "Just wait until I regain my strength," he says, climbing back on the bike and taking off down the street.

Driving through, he passes souls making their decision, the rest continuing to meander aimlessly. As Murdio is about to drive through the city, he comes upon a block of houses off the main road. He turns the bike down the street and rolls down it slowly, looking at the buildings. He pauses as he finds a spirit perched on a handrail of one of a building, staring into the sky.

It looks down at him before back to the sky. "You're from up there," the spirits whispers, floating off the rail to the steps.

"Yes, I am," Murdio says.

The spirit's eyes widen as it stops on the steps, watching Murdio dismount his motorcycle.

"You must not speak of that," the spirit whispers, trying to place his hand on the rail.

"Why not?" Murdio asks. He looks around as rumbling shakes the ground.

"You've brought them here!" the spirit says in a panic, floating up the stairs, and through the door to safety. "This way!"

Murdio looks down the road, seeing the hood of a bone-vehicle with a skeleton driving. He turns back, seeing the door open, allowing him inside. Murdio leaves the bike against the building and jumps over the handrail, getting to the door. Once through, Murdio stops and turns back with his hand out. The metallic gold peels off and floats, forming a staff just as the door closes. Murdio rushes to the window alongside the spirit, looking outside. He holds his breath as the street trembles when the transport moves forward. It comes to a stop in the street in front of the house, the driver's skull moving around.

Suddenly, two skeletons appear, looking around before pointing to a building in the distance. The two drop back inside as the vehicle moves closer.

Murdio watches as the driver lifts a bone from inside the console. Another round of rumbling occurs when a skull rises from the roof. The skull's jaw drops, firing a projectile into a building nearby. The impact sends a rattling explosion high into the sky. Shockwaves send debris around it, knocking Murdio to the floor. As he gets to his feet, he looks out, noticing the orange glow.

Flames lick the building as the vehicle vanishes from sight. To Murdio's surprise, the flames dwindle quickly, the building knitting itself back together. "What is this?" Murdio mutters in confusion.

"The magic of Thinker road," the spirit answers.

Murdio steps back, turning to the source. "Thinker road?" Murdio says.

"We are the philosophers of this world," it replies.

Murdio nods as it turns, moving into another room. Murdio follows it, finding a group of spirits sitting along the wall.

"So, we agree on sanctuary?" the spirit says, making its way to the others. The rest nod when they turn to Murdio.

"Thinker Brendan, who is this?" another spirit says.

"Murdio, from above," Brendan says, surprising Murdio. Silence fills the air, the spirits inspecting Murdio carefully.

"How can we be sure this is the real Murdio?" one asks, floating toward Murdio.

"Erik, how dare you question him!" Brendan snaps, stepping toward him.

Murdio steps closer, looking him in the face. "I'll show you my truth," Murdio says, dropping the staff. Just as it hits the floor, Murdio's ragged and dirty clothes fade, his armor returning.

Erik retreats, looking down at Murdio's feet. "My apologies, I am skeptical from life here," Erik mumbles hesitantly.

"This is true, I have known him in life," a spirit says, wisping above the ground.

"Always so helpful, Joan," Erik says, looking into its colorless face.

Murdio smirks, grabbing the staff in his hand and returning his façade.

"Where are your halo and wings?" Erik asks.

"Taken from me," Murdio growls.

"How does one lose them?" Brendan asks softly.

"A spear of corruption entered my sanctuary," Murdio says, flashing back to that time.

"In Heaven?" Joan asks, breaking Murdio from his own mind.

"Of course, it happened in Heaven," Erik snapped, turning from Joan to Murdio. "So, what are you doing here?"

Before Murdio answers, Brendan walks towards Erik, whispering into his ear.

Erik turns to Brendan, who nods back at him while the rest look on.

"What is it?" Joan asks curiously. She then watches him float over, beginning to whisper to her.

"The halo you are looking for is hidden in the heart of Demoza," Erik says.

"Where is that?" Murdio asks, surprised that they know of his quest.

"Beyond the horizon," Erik says, turning to the window.

"Then that is where I will go," Murdio replies, following the spirit's gaze.

"Then what are you going to do?" asks another voice from behind him.

Murdio turns, finding a spirit that was taller than the others. "Get my divinity back."

"And how do you plan to get the item you seek?" the spirit asks.

"By force," Murdio says simply. Truthfully, he hadn't thought that far yet.

The being smirks, walking through Murdio before he stops in front of the others.

"For being God's son, he sure doesn't think things through," he says derisively.

"Well Patrig, he may be God's son, but he is not like us," Brendan says, a slight admonition in his voice.

"You have a point," Patrig says, looking back at Murdio.

Murdio steps back as the Thinkers come together against the wall. "What are your roles here?" Murdio asks, looking at each of them.

Patrig looks over at Brendan before turning back to Murdio. "We aid any lost soul."

Murdio leans against a wall as they stand, as a soul slowly floating into the room.

"Welcome, how may we provide you direction?" Erik asks.

"My greed screams for the Fallen, however, I prefer sanctuary," the spirit says, beginning to regain some of his humanly features.

"Only you may make the final judgment, we can only assist with any confliction," Joan says gently.

"Let us see where you stand," Patrig says, moving toward the spirit.

The ghost floats in silence, watching Patrig lean back and then plunge his hand into its chest. The spirit watches as Patrig's hand begins releasing the energies of both dark and light. The energies circle each other inside the ghost as Patrig waits with his eyes shut. While Murdio and the others watch in silence, the glowing disappears, allowing Patrig to remove his hand.

Patrig floats back toward the others, opening his eyes to look at the spirit.

"What is your judgment?" the ghost asks hopefully, shifting his eyes to Patrig.

"You must relinquish your positivity or ask for forgiveness for the sins during your life," Patrig says.

"Once all is in alignment, they will come," Brendan says, walking to Patrig's side.

"Understood," the ghost replies before disappearing into the ceiling.

"I must return to my redemption," Murdio says, beginning to turn away. He is surprised when all the Thinkers turn in unison to look at him.

"Do you think you're ready?" Erik asks, causing Murdio to stop in his tracks.

"Do you even know where you are going?" Patrig continues.

Murdio looks toward the front door. "All I know is that I must return to my home."

Murdio steps toward the door, leaving them floating in silence. He swings the door open, making his way outside into the currently tranquil surroundings. Continuing down the stairs, Murdio looks over to where the central part of town where souls remain on their pathway. At the bottom step, he finds the rusty motorcycle frame, leaning where he left it. He approaches it, pulling the staff from his back. It glows as he steps to the bike, which rattles and shakes as the staff merges into the frame. Murdio mounts up and turns it toward the main road, looking back up at the open doorway.

The Thinkers watch in silence as Murdio proceeds back to the road.

As the sound echoes through the emptiness, Murdio finds himself on a familiar street. To his right, Murdio finds a Fallen vehicle in the street, a skeleton soliciting assistance from the wandering souls.

"This must be stopped," Murdio whispers, turning his bike toward them. Murdio revs the engine, catching the skeleton's attention as he accelerates forward.

A mass of the creatures begins to pour from the vehicle, the skeletons gathering up their weapons. Darkness drips from their blades onto the broke pavement like water from a leaky pipe.

Murdio speeds toward them, surprising them when he jumps backward, the bike continuing to accelerate between the skeletons and the transport vehicle. The collision causes an explosion, the vehicles erupting into flames, sending shards of bones into the building around the area. As the smoke continues to rise into the air, red eyes pierce through the smoke.

"You have no power here," the skeleton says, its voice rough like gravel.

Murdio remains silent as he strides toward them, unafraid of their evil glares.

"Here is a taste of darkness!" another skeleton yells, charging Murdio, his weapon overhead.

Murdio stops and places his hands out, liquid gold streaking out of the burning carcass of the vehicle. The liquid squeezes between the openings in his fingers and solidifies into the staff. Murdio smirks, pushing the attack upward with a thrust, knocking the skeleton off balance. He swings to the right, changing his grip, swinging his staff hard at the skeleton's neck. The staff strikes it, leaving a trail of gold dripping from Murdio's weapon. The skeleton tumbles, crashing into the wreckage, sending a ball of flames upwards. The other closes its lower jaw, turning to Murdio as his gold staff continues to solidify into shape.

"You will pay for that!" the skeleton screams as the flames disappear, leaving nothing but the ashes on the street. The skeleton's eyes begin to glow, its weapon infusing with flames from the wreckage.

"You can either suffer the same or tell me where I may find what I am looking for," says Murdio, the final drop of gold hitting the street.

"How about I destroy you and clear the way for Fallen victory?" the skeleton bellows, flames shooting out of its grin.

Murdio and the skeleton rush toward one another with weapons high. Their arms collide, releasing flames and light, stopping each other in their tracks with the force of their blows. As a thin layer of ash settles from the sky, Murdio finds himself face-to-skull with the skeleton, locked in a stalemate. The two pull away, attempting to find a way to try another attack.

"Don't you know who I am?" Murdio challenges, watching the flames hang from the skeleton's body.

"I do," the skeleton says mockingly.

"How could you have?" Murdio asks, sensing that this creature knew more than it should.

"I am Turmal," it says. "I sent the demon to corrupt you!"

Murdio angrily charges Turmal, but before he can reach the creature, it disappears. Murdio looks around, finding no sign, only emptiness. "Come out you coward!" Murdio yells. He suddenly feels a shadow towering over him.

"You're coming with me!" Turmal says, suddenly striking the back of Murdio's head, knocking him out.

CHAPTER FIVE
Behind Fallen Lines

MURDIO OPENS HIS EYES, unable to move his arms. Finding himself bound, Murdio looks to see a twisting chain. Murdio turns back, his breath frosting in the air, behind bars of ice. "Where am I?" Murdio says, struggling to get free.

"At the Fallen fortress," another prisoner replies, echoing off the icy walls.

Murdio looks down at the chain, struggling to stand upon an icy floor. Just as he gets to his feet, his chains tighten, sending Murdio grimacing to his knees. "How did I get here?" he asks, groaning in pain. Murdio draws a ragged breath as the chain loosens back to normal.

Before the other prisoner can answer, a skeleton creeps along the outside of the cage, holding an item gleaming in the light. "Welcome, Murdio, to your final resting place," the skeleton growls.

"I will break free of these, and then escape from here," Murdio says, struggling to get free. He stopped, looking around for his staff.

"Looking for this?" the skeleton taunted, stepping aside and revealing the golden staff frozen within an icicle.

Murdio's eyes widen, fear filling him. "Give it back, or I shall make you pray for a painless judgment," Murdio snarls, struggling to get back to his feet. He manages to grab the bars, feeling the cold stinging his hands.

"You fool, your Father carries no power in this world," the fallen says.

"I will get out of here," Murdio says, slamming his fists against the ice.

The skeleton laughs, walking away from Murdio's cell. The sound of his laughter fades and the silence returns as Murdio stares at his frozen staff.

He reaches his hands out to try to summon the staff from its frozen tomb. As his hands shake from concentrating, the staff bounces inside its icy chamber, desperate to break free. Murdio's hope slips and he lets the staff go still. He presses his head against the icy bars, dropping his hands, giving up.

"They will never let you out of here," a voice calls.

Murdio turns around, catching sight of something between the bars. "I will escape, besides how could you know?" Murdio asks, making his way to the bars between the two cells.

"The only way you get out is when they need you," the stranger says, stepping into the light.

Murdio jumps back, seeing all the wounds that cover his body from head to toe. "How have you been able to survive this torment?" Murdio asks, suddenly afraid.

"A refusal to give into demons, knowing that my Father will provide sanctuary," the stranger replies. He points toward his cell door and Murdio realizes it's not closed.

"Your cage ... it's open ... you're free," Murdio says, disbelief and confusion in his voice. He turns his attention to the stranger.

The stranger shakes his head and drops into the shadows out of Murdio's view. Murdio can hear his ragged breathing, the only sound in the total emptiness of the dungeon.

"I cannot, for you see, I have lost faith," the stranger says from the shadows.

"God will never leave you," Murdio says emphatically.

The stranger steps into the light once again, looking down at the icy floor. "Have you not realized that God does not exist in this world?" the stranger whispers.

"God is everywhere and is only a prayer away," Murdio says. Suddenly the bars separating the two cells disappear, leaving the them face-to-face.

"You are foolish if you think God will always guide you to prosperity," the stranger scoffs, lifting his face into the light.

Murdio stares at the stranger. Fear turns his blood cold as he realizes, underneath the wounds and old scars, the stranger is him. "Who are you?" Murdio demands, taking another step backward.

"I am you," the stranger says, a twisted smile coming to his face. "If you continue to hold firm to your beliefs."

"Blasphemy!" Murdio yells angrily. "My Father will never let that become truth!"

The stranger glides over, grabbing Murdio and lifting him up by the collar of his shirt. "Then you and your power will waste away inside this dungeon," the stranger says as Murdio struggles against him.

"Who are you really?" Murdio demands, trying to loosen his grip.

"You," the stranger replies, suddenly disappearing.

Murdio gasps as he finds himself alone again. "That nightmare will never come," Murdio says to the emptiness, looking around, finding no cells besides his own.

Around him, walls of ice trap him inside even as the dagger-like icicle sits alone. Murdio looks down, beginning to feel a chill, the silence suffocating. He catches the bars to steady himself on the ice-floor, shivering against the cold. He stared hopelessly at his reflection in the icicle, looking up at the sound of footsteps.

The two skeletons make their way into the dungeon, leaving a massive creature alone in the doorway. Catching a glimpse of it, Murdio makes out the creature's fleshy skin giving way to the dense bone. The skeletons give a grin when suddenly the beast raises an enormous hammer, sending it crashing down. The vibration shakes the icicles on the roof free, sending them shattering to the floor.

Murdio staggers back, looking toward his ice-encased staff. The frosty air thins, allowing Murdio to watch in horror as the creature takes hold of the staff. The skeletons turn, finding Murdio watching every movement of the staff.

"Strength can only get you so far," the creature growls, beginning to test the weapon's durability.

"Yeah, and what would you know of it?" Murdio demands. He opens his hands, attempting to summon the staff from the beast's grip.

Before he can, the skeletons charge toward him, trying to stop him. Murdio manages to dodge their grasp and retreats to the back of his cell, trying once more. The skeletons are unable to reach him beyond the bars, allowing him to regain control.

The creature struggles to keep hold of the staff, watching as it tears itself from its hands. The staff barrels forward at Murdio's call, between the two skeletons, sliding easily between the bars of the cell.

"Quickly, tighten the chains!" the beast commands.

The two scurry toward a dark chain that connects Murdio to the cell. They grab hold as the staff returning to Murdio's hands. Suddenly, the chain pulses violently, tightening around Murdio.

Murdio falls to the ground, struggling to keep a steady grip on his staff. He tries to take a deep breath as he falls over, exacerbating the pain.

"We're winning, Geral," the skeleton says, turning toward the other. They look over at Murdio, seeing him move to his knees, groaning in pain.

"Not just yet, Murus," the second skeleton says.

Murdio yells suddenly, jamming the staff through the layers of ice on the floor. He rises to his feet as a jagged crack zig-zags across the room.

The skeletons turn back to the chain, trying to tighten its hold to weaken Murdio. They watch as the charge of darkness fails.

Murdio turns to the chain and catches it in his fist. He throws the chain into the wall behind him, pulling it through the bars, sending the skeletons crashing through the icicle bars. As the shards of ice settle, the skeletons slide across the icy floor into the wall, landing on top of the links of chain.

"Now it's you and me," Murdio says, his breathing returning to normal. Behind him, the skeletons lay broken on the rubble.

"Not exactly," the monster, Senob, replies.

Murdio watches two more skeletons appear from the doorway. He turns his attention back to Senob, charging at the monster with rage. He leaps over the shards of ice left from the cell door, diving upon Senob's muscular girth.

Before Murdio can unleash a strike, Senob grabs his hammer, swinging it into Murdio's chest. The blow sends shockwaves rippling through his skin, throwing him into the wall amongst the broken bones. With a thud, Murdio collapses, struggling to draw another breath. Senob looks on as the two new skeletons step toward Murdio's unmoving body.

They bend down, turning Murdio over onto his back, seeing the discoloration on his still face.

"Is he dead?" one asks, poking Murdio's shoulder.

"It doesn't matter, bring him to the main chamber," Senob commands, pointing out toward the darkness.

"Yes, General Senob," the skeleton says, grabbing hold of Murdio's limbs.

Murdio's body in hand, the skeletons drag him out the door and out of Senob's sight. Before Senob walks out, he throws down the bludgeoning hammer, which sticks into the ground. Suddenly, Senob sees a faint glimmer underneath the mound of bones near where Murdio fell. Senob cautiously walks over, finding the golden staff. Senob kneels down, wrapping his skinless fingers around it.

"Murdio's staff," Senob says to himself, holding it in his hands. With a smirk, Senob walks out of the room, following after the skeletons. He finds them at the bottom of the stairway to his chamber.

Inside the chamber, Senob walks toward his seat, a chair perched on a platform of bones. He watches as the skeletons drop Murdio on the floor.

Murdio's eyes slowly open, Senob's image growing clearer. Before Murdio can fully regain consciousness, the two skeletons grab his shoulders, forcing him to his knees.

"Stay down," the skeletons say, pressing down on Murdio's arms.

Murdio shakes off the skeleton, taking in the emptiness around him. Blood splatters cover the walls and floors, forcing Murdio to turn to Senob.

"Come Forseer and Lukas" Senob says, holding up Murdio's golden staff tauntingly. Murdio watches as Senob motions two skeleton soldiers into the room. His attention shifts to another figure dragging itself inside the room ahead of another.

"Come Forseer and Lukas," Senob commands.

The one behind dragging itself, Murdio noticing its bones were heavily damaged with large cracks threading through it. They glance at Murdio as they cross to stand by Senob, awaiting his orders.

"I pray to you Holy Father for their forgiveness," Murdio whispers, bowing his head.

"Prayers to your Father mean nothing to us," Senob growls.

"Believe me he is stubborn in his faith," the Foreseer says, turning to Senob.

"What does a heathen know about faith?" Murdio demands.

"You watch your tone," the skeleton behind Senob says.

"No, Lukas, I want him to know," the Foreseer says.

"God's ears hear even the faintest prayers," Senob sneers sarcastically, looking over to the Foreseer.

"I dare him to involve himself," the Foreseer says, causing Senob to turn his attention to him. "He no longer knows who I am."

"Who cares who you are?" Murdio demands. "Fallen scum!"

The Foreseer steps forward, pulling back his hood.

Murdio watches as the shadows peel away, revealing the face of a human around the burning fire in its eyes.

"Underneath the Foreseer façade is Velkaun," Senob says, raising his hand to Velkaun.

"What has become of you?" Murdio asks.

"Senob has shown me the stupidity that is faith," Velkaun replies, looking over at Senob.

"The only stupidity is embracing a false prophet such as Senob," Murdio says.

"Enough banter," Senob yells.

Velkaun places his hood back up, casting his flesh into darkness. He then lowers his head, stepping back to Senob's side.

Taking advantage of the weakening pressure over him, Murdio rises and charges at Velkaun. Before Murdio can get close, Lukas delivers a punch to his midsection which sends Murdio to his knees. Clutching his ribs, Murdio watches Lukas step back to his post behind Senob. His eyes blurry with tears, Murdio watches the two skeletons make their way around him. Unable to fight back, he kneels helplessly as they drag him back.

"You are truly one blinded soul," Senob says, standing from the throne, staff in hand. Senob steps toward him, beginning to twirl it within the bits of flesh around his bones.

Murdio watches Senob kneel, bringing his ugly face close to Murdio's.

"That dedication will be my light," Murdio growls, trying to shake off the skeletons' grip once more. Their boney hands shake, digging harder into his skin.

Senob smirks as Murdio continues to clench in pain. "I'm so scared, I'm shaking in my decayed flesh," Senob says, causing the others to chuckle. Senob's smile vanishes, looking at the staff as he grasps it with both hands. He then turns to Lukas, nodding at an unspoken command.

Lukas shifts his palms downward, allowing darkening shadows to release into the floor below. The walls begin to rattle as a pillar rises from the demonic energy. Once the pillar is complete, the quaking ceases.

Senob turns toward it, pulling the staff behind his head. Then, as Murdio watches, Senob swings with all his might at the pillar, the staff ringing as it strikes the cold, hard stone. Despite all his strength, Senob is surprised to find the staff intact.

"Did you really think that was going to work?" Murdio says, chuckling at Senob's apparent frustration.

"Silence your gospel," Senob snaps, attempting a second strike. Once more, the staff rings with the blow, but is unharmed. Senob brings the staff closer, frustrated that there is no sign of even a scratch.

"Truly a piece of undying faith," Murdio says confidently. Once more, Murdio attempts to break the skeletons' hold.

"Indeed, however, it cannot withstand our force," Senob says calmly. The dark matter making up the pillar implodes, sending the darkness spreading into the cracks of the flooring. Senob makes his way back to his throne between Lukas and Velkaun.

"Sir, we can destroy it together," Lukas says, his hands wrapping in violet flames.

Senob nods, giving the staff to Lukas.

Lukas grips the staff firmly and turns toward Velkaun, dropping the other end of the staff into his hands. As the two each take hold, their own energies begin to take hold inside the golden metal. Murdio watches in horror as the gold start to break apart.

Senob stands, his grin returning as golden flakes fall to the floor. "See? Eventually, despair and torment take control," Senob says. He walks toward to Velkaun and Lukas.

Murdio watches as their energies swirling around the staff's center, crippling the metal base. Senob snatches the staff from out of their grasps, surprising them and Murdio.

"Forgive them, Father, they don't know what they do," Murdio prays in despair.

"Your verses carry no weight!" Senob snaps, watching Velkaun summon another pillar from the darkness.

"Let's show him our real power," Velkaun says.

"I may have had a change of heart," Senob replies, pointing his finger between his sternum.

Velkaun looks on in confusion but lowers his hands, causing the pillar to implode.

Senob looks at the staff before glancing at Murdio. Senob then grasps hold of one side, beginning to lift it over his head. With no hesitation, he cracks it swiftly over his knee, holding a piece of the staff in each hand.

Murdio bites his tongue to remain silent, watching as Senob admires his results. Stricken, Murdio can only watch as Senob turns to Velkaun and Lukas, a single piece in each hand.

Senob extends them to Velkaun and Lukas, staring down at the crumbling halves.

Lukas and Velkaun grab hold, beginning the absorb the metal into their bones.

"What shall we do with this power?" Velkaun asks, examining his hand.

"None of my concern," Senob replies, causing Velkaun and Lukas to bow to him. Velkaun turns to Lukas before falling into a massive pool beneath him. Once out of sight, Lukas turns to Senob, pointing out the opening.

"Try to at least clear the opening," Senob says.

"I wasn't even thinking of doing it again," Lukas says shortly.

They watch as fire begins to ignite from his back, taking the shape of demonic wings.

"Just trying to maintain its integrity," Senob orders, watching Lukas's wings extend outward.

Lukas looks back to Murdio, who doesn't meet his eyes. "Pathetic," Lukas chuckles, suddenly bursting through the roof, sending rubble toward the ground.

Senob turns to Murdio. "So the 'son of God', how does it feel to be weak?" he taunts.

Murdio's head drops without an answer and Senob roars with laughter as he turns toward his throne.

However, before he can get far, Murdio's body suddenly convulses, allowing a holy light to emanate from him. The guards struggle to keep him still as Murdio drops to the ground, engulfed in glowing light.

Senob watches Murdio explode into a ball of light, unable to move. The shockwave sends the two skeleton guards crashing into the wall, leaving Murdio free. Gulping down fear, Senob turns back, staring into Murdio's eyes.

"I don't know," Murdio roars, the light beginning to fade.

Murdio reaches for Senob, stopping when the sound of bones clattering rings out. He pauses, seeing one of the guards stumbling back to its feet. When Murdio turns back around, he realizes Senob has disappeared.

"Don't forget about us," one of the guards says, using his other hand to reattach his forearm.

Murdio looks at them before running from the room, following the fading sound of Senob's footsteps. The two guards give chase and Murdio slides behind an ice fragment, watching them pass him.

"Believe me, I didn't," Murdio says, jumping from his hiding spot and sending a massive vibration into the ground. The skeletons brace themselves as spear-like icicles come crashing down from the ceiling. Once the final icicle shatters, the two look around with skeletal grins.

"You missed us," one of the skeletons says.

Murdio says nothing as the ground collapses, sending them tumbling into a pit. Murdio looks around the room, once again hearing the faint sound of footsteps. He then runs to the hole in the floor, seeing Senob making his way out of the fortress. Without hesitation, Murdio jumps through the hole to stop him.

Senob pauses as Murdio falls, landing feet first upon the skeletal remains. He covers his eyes as the dust swirls around him, frozen with fear. "You can't catch me," Senob screams, suddenly turning toward a nearby vehicle.

Murdio bends down, sending his hand through the sand as Senob sprints away. After a second of ruffling, his hand pulls out a sharp bone, which he throws at Senob.

Just before Senob can reach for the vehicle's door, the bone slams into the rib of the car, within an inch of his skull. Senob looks back at Murdio in fear.

Murdio slowly walks toward Senob. As he gets closer, Senob shakes his head, going for the door once more. As Senob twists the handle and climbs inside, Murdio lunges for the vehicle. He surprises Senob when he reaches out, grabbing Senob's spine through the rib bones of the car.

"Tell me where I need to go," Murdio commands, tightening his fingers around Senob's vertebrae.

"No amount of divine intervention can make me!" Senob yells defiantly, trying to break Murdio's hold.

Murdio squeezes, tossing Senob away from the controls. He then rips the door from its hinges, allowing him to make his way inside.

Senob quickly tries to pick himself up.

"Tell me where I can find my staff," Murdio says, kneeling next to Senob.

"I will never tell you," Senob splutters.

Senob surprises Murdio when he regains his footing, charging at Murdio. The impact sends them into the side of the vehicle, rocking it. Senob gathers himself, looking at Murdio's motionless body next to shards of bone. He paces around Murdio, his eyes landing on a broken femur. Senob kneels, picking it up off the ground, keeping Murdio in his periphery.

With a smirk, Senob walks to Murdio's side, the bone suddenly darkening. Senob lifts the weapon and drives it into Murdio's chest. Just as the bone pierces Murdio's skin, a light erupts, surrounding it.

Murdio's eyes open as Senob steps back, the bone remaining inside his chest. Murdio rises from the floor as Senob struggles to escape. Murdio reaches down and rips the bone from his chest. Throwing it down, the wound fills with light as Murdio turns his attention to Senob.

"I forgive you," Murdio says gently, "for you know not what you do."

"I hope your father can forgive me for this," Senob replies, charging at Murdio once again.

Murdio sidesteps, sending Senob crashing through the vehicle's side. Senob gets back to his feet as Murdio watches on, the glow faintly remaining all around. Senob cracks his knuckles and vertebrae as he begins to step toward Murdio. Before he can make it any further, an object crashes in front of Senob.

As Murdio looks all around, Senob kneels to check the object.

"Is this some trickery of your own creation?" Murdio says, trying to make out the object just of Senob's reach.

Senob squints, pulling up from the sand a glowing rock. "Another piece of divine intervention?" Senob demands, throwing the rock away.

A spirit suddenly floats down, landing between Murdio and Senob. Murdio recognizes it to be Patrig, while Senob struggles to comprehend what's happening.

"Nice to see you again," Murdio says, grinning at the ghost.

"Who do you think you are?" Senob screams.

Patriq smirks, disappearing from either's view before reappearing behind Murdio. "Don't you remember us," Patrig replies, revealing the other spirits of the group.

Furious, Senob begins to shake in anger, his hands darkening in rage. As the darkness drips from his hands, it swirls into a whirlpool at his feet.

After the whirlpool calms, the shadows release toward Murdio, slithering forward. Just as Murdio braces himself, the shadows curve around him, dropping beneath the free spirits. Before they can move, claws appear, grabbing hold of the spirits, trying to drag them down. As they begin to squirm, arrows rain down from the sky beyond the clouds. The arrows fly through the air, crashing into the shadows, causing them to dissipate from sight.

"Now what?!" Senob yells, lifting his arms into the air.

A beam erupts from the clouds, a being suddenly floating down. Her wings drape down on either side, blonde hair falling perfectly between them. She continues to descend, holding a bow dripping gold in her hands. She lands in the sand, which flutters around her feet, leaving everyone in awe. As they continue to look on, the being walks in front of the spirits, looking up to the glowing sky. The spirits, extending their wings, lift off the ground and fly off into the open air.

"Another angel joins the fray," Senob sneers, watching her focus on him.

Murdio leans over to the angel as she stares upon Senob, silently awaiting their next move. "What are you doing here?" he whispers.

"My name is Annabelle, and I am a guardian angel," she says, allowing her bow to shine in her light.

Senob kneels before grabbing a rib cage in one hand and a solid bone in another. He jams the bone into the sternum, charging at Murdio. Before he can get any closer, Annabelle grabs an arrow from the quiver on her back, placing the arrow in the bow. Before Senob can strike, the arrow pierces the center of his left eye socket, erupting from the back of his skull. The arrow spins away, vanishing as bone fragments rain down behind him. Senob screams in terror, lifting his hand to cover the eye.

Murdio and Annabelle look at each other. "I'm sure you can get what you need now," Annabelle says, saluting with her bow, extending her wings. With a single flap, she takes off into the sky, leaving Murdio and Senob alone on the barren land.

"So typical of an angel to hit and run," Senob mutters, removing his hand.

"Just like a Fallen to blame someone else," Murdio replies, flexing his hands. Murdio then watches as Senob lifts his head, revealing the open hole.

"She will pay once I finish with you," Senob yells, throwing his hands down.

"She was always handy with arrows," Murdio replies, watching Senob kneel down.

Senob grabs hold of his bone club, charging Murdio, swinging his club. Before the club can get close, Murdio dodges, beginning to spread his arms out, hands shut. While Senob recovers his balance, Murdio opens his hands, bringing them together. The impact sends a shockwave of sand rippling around them. After a few seconds, Murdio looks at his hands in confusion, Senob laughing at him.

"Did I not tell you that you have no powers on this ground?" Senob says, laughing as the sand settles.

Shortly after, larger chunks fall from the sky, landing all around Senob's feet. The light dims, causing Senob to look up into the darkening sky. From above, a large chunk of floor crashes down on Senob, sending dust and bone upwards.

Once the dust clears, Murdio watches the remains of the flooring crumble on top of Senob's remains. Murdio walks to the rubble, kneeling and lifting one of the smaller pieces away. To his surprise, Murdio finds Senob's skull dragging itself out. Murdio watches it boost itself upright.

With cracks and chips, the skull sits before Murdio. "You are going to fail," the skull chuckles, as the cracks continue to widen.

"As long as I have faith, I am never alone," Murdio says, kneeling down, reaching for the top of the skull. Despite its frugal attempt, Murdio lifts the skull as it tries to bite his hands.

"Foolish son of the Holy One," the skull yells, Murdio throws the head deep within the crater.

CHAPTER SIX
Balancing the Odds

MURDIO STANDS AND TURNS around, his eyes landing on two towers of light in the distance. He looks at the bone-vehicle, jumping inside and looking around for an ignition. As he begins to dig around, light through the roof causes a single panel to glow. Moving closer, Murdio sees a single lever. With a bit of hesitance, Murdio extends his hand, grasping the lever. The bones shake violently, causing the bottom to open. As Murdio watches, a golden pedestal lifts from behind the meaty dashboard.

On top, a single skull sits silently. Murdio approaches, keeping his guard up. He jiggles the skull, trying to make it move to no avail. Finally, out of anger, he swipes at it, causing it to lean forward, the vehicle charging forward. Struggling to brace himself, he finds the skull remaining steady. With his hand firmly on each side, Murdio extends his hand, attempting to slow down. Before he can lose his grip, he strikes it back into position, sending the vehicle to a stop.

Dizzy, he stumbles toward the opening to poke his head outside. Looking around, Murdio watches as the spinning world settles enough to reveal the lack of movement. He then turns the other direction, finding two beams pulsing upwards.

"I am coming," Murdio says, ducking his head back inside. After a brief pause, he lifts his hand to the top of the skull. His fingers grip the holes inside, the skull rising from the pedestal. To his surprise, the bones cause the frame to break apart, causing the vehicle to lose shape. Murdio keeps the skull steady, watching the movement cease. Murdio raises the skull above his head, causing the bones to float into the open air. After a quick glimpse, he turns the skull around, placing it down in the direction of the light.

It locks into place, the sockets glowing red as vessels tangle themselves around the skull from the floorboards. Attaching to the bones, they reconstruct piece by piece. As Murdio watches, the vessels create the frame, locking the bones together. Once the last one was in place, Murdio cautiously makes his way to the platform, sitting in the front. A single window allows him to see the outside world.

Murdio turns to the skull as the red sockets begin to go dim. As Murdio turns to the opening, he places a hand near the eyes, pushing his hand forward. The vehicle takes off toward the beams, shedding the sand coating it. Murdio watches as the building disappears, nothing else developing close by. Even as the speed increases, Murdio's eyes bounce all over, looking to break the monotony of sandy ground. After some time, Murdio pauses, allowing his eyes to focus in on a sparkling light. Trying to make out the source, Murdio's hand slips, sending the vehicle screaming down the road.

Murdio manages to break the spell of the light, regaining a hold on the skull. He pushes it, causing the vehicle to slow down, lessening the waves of sand around it. Regaining his composure, Murdio turns his attention back to the window, finding a twisting pillar of energy spinning sand upwards into the clouds. Murdio pulls back on the skull further, causing the vehicle screech to a halt. Before it can come to a complete stop, Murdio crashes into the window when the vehicle crashes to a halt. Murdio opens his eyes, looking out of the broken glass, seeing the entire bone structure in front of him. Murdio locates a crevice inside of the bones, causing him to rip the skull from its pedestal. Murdio then throws it into the heart of the break, causing it to splinter outwards.

"Wow," Murdio says, examining the structure when it shatters, sending pieces to the ground. He steps through the frame into the sand and the bright sun.

Murdio walks around to the front, finding a dent in the front of the vehicle. Inches from it, a rusting pole extends from the sand. At the top sits a board splintering in the wind. Murdio walks up to the board, catching fragments behind a coating of sand. Murdio wipes the board, revealing the rusty surface beneath as the sand breaks off. As the sunlight strikes the surface, the fragments begin to come together. Going letter by letter, Murdio manages to make out the wording on the sign.

"Heaven," Murdio whispers, reading all the way to the end. Murdio's eyes find a faint word scrawled across the bottom. "NO."

"Ironic that a place such as this shares the name of Father's kingdom," a voice echoes from the wind.

Murdio discovers an angelic woman, floating above the sand. "Annabelle?"

The angel nods, sinking into the sand even as her wings drape over it.

"What happened here?" Murdio asks, watching Annabelle approach, staring at the sign in silence.

After a moment, Annabelle to look back at Murdio. "A loss of faith in humanity," Annabelle says, looking over to the sign, placing her hand gently against its surface. A tear forms, rolling down her pristine cheek into the emptiness below.

Murdio looks past her, taking in the sight of ruins lying beyond the sign. As the wind swirls, Murdio's emotions sour, causing despair to grip into his heart.

"This is what transpires when humans lose faith in everything," Annabelle says, placing her hand on Murdio's shoulder.

Murdio's eyes remain on the destruction, struggling to speak. "How can that happen when they are built in God's image?" Murdio says, feeling her hand lift off his shoulder. Murdio turns, finding Annabelle approaching the sign, resting her head on the edge of the sign.

"Tested by sin, resulting in the inability to comprehend the answers, deepening the darkness," Annabelle says.

Murdio's fists tighten, struggling to find a way to stop the tears behind his eyes. Murdio reopens his eyes, turning his attention to the ruins, leaving Annabelle statuesque with her golden hair down her back. "I will restore the faith and belief." The clouds break, allowing a stream of light downward next to Annabelle.

Annabelle nods as the light warms her feet. She shifts, turning back to Murdio with a small smile before stepping into the light and disappearing in its shine.

Once again alone, Murdio breathes and begins to take his first step, turning his attention to the ruins. After a while, Murdio continues to stare when he feels the sand slip from underneath his feet. He instantly stops, looking down, finding a dark trench separating him from the ruins. He looks left and then right, finding no means to cross.

Murdio turns his attention back to the trench, getting lost in the pitch-black darkness, his mind wondering at the mysterious evils that will come before him. He jumps back when, out of the darkness, demon hands lift from the strange surface, grasping at the air.

Murdio steps back further, looking around as they squirm, attempting to grab anything within reach. The movement ceases as they vanish below the rippling surface, causing it to calm. The darkness starts to tremble, churning waves onto the sandy coastline. Murdio retreats, the darkness revealing a patch of dry sand nearby. Murdio watches the waves start to build themselves into staircases on both sides of the trench. The staircase fluctuates before stopping and solidifying.

Murdio places a foot on the first step. Besides a bit of a bend in the shadowy formation, the stairs hold up beneath his weight. Step by step, Murdio makes his way to the bottom of the trench, standing between walls of shadows. The dark hands reappear out of the sides of both the walls, causing Murdio to jump. When he sees that they aren't coming closer, he continues toward the bottom of the staircase. Each step closer, Murdio avoids their grasp, wiggling around the walls top to bottom. Before he can step, the top stair liquefies as it crawls up to the sandy coast. Murdio remains frozen near the lower level, a shadowy figure rising from out of the cloudy liquid. Murdio's eyes widen as he watches Lukas take form, half of his staff still in his hand.

"Well if it isn't the mighty Murdio," Lukas says, lifting the staff higher into Murdio's view.

"Give me your half, and your punishment will not be painful," Murdio commands, suddenly watching demonic hands appear and grab hold of his feet.

"I am shaking in my boots," Lukas taunts, watching Murdio struggle to break free from the hands' grasp.

Murdio bends down, using his hands to pry them open. He manages to get loose, looking at Lukas, finding him mysteriously gone. Murdio charges up the stairs, hoping that he can still catch Lukas before he vanishes. However, as he gets to the sandy bottom, Murdio finds no sign of him, only the ruins in the distance. Suddenly, the sand vibrates again, and Murdio whips around to see the darkness break loose and meld itself together.

"No going back," he says to himself.

"You didn't forget about me, did you?" Lukas's voice sounds.

Murdio spins around, trying to find Lukas. "Where are you, coward?"

"Here let me help you," Lukas replies.

Before Murdio can speak, a light momentarily appears near the ruins before going dark. "Why don't you come back so we can handle this once and for all?" Murdio calls, trying to find another way to get to that side.

"That wouldn't be fun," Lukas taunts. "Besides I have a better idea." Once the darkness dissipates, a blinding speck of light lifts into the sky.

Struggling to keep it in view, Murdio watches the light fly overhead before crashing within the ruins. "When I find it, Lukas, I will come for the other piece."

"Good luck," Lukas replies, gurgling into silence.

Murdio takes in the scene, seeing only darkness and emptiness. Keeping an eye out for the staff, he approaches the edges of the broken city. As he gets closer, Murdio finds himself taken in by a dense fog. He looks around, watching as the fog sinks in a mist of darkness. He steps toward the road between the buildings, feeling the fog weighing upon his shoulders.

Eventually, Murdio spots a light piercing the fog on the other side of the road. He rushes toward it, watching as the light scurries randomly through the fog. "Wait for me." Then to his surprise, the light expands as he gets within reach, the fog continuing to get heavier.

"Murdio?" a voice calls from within the light, causing the particles to remain still.

"I'm here," Murdio says, standing in front of the light.

"Why have you come here?"

"Matters beyond understanding," Murdio says.

"I can provide some assistance," the voice echoes, allowing specks of light to cascade into the sky. As they gather together, the lights start to rise above Murdio circling throughout the sky before streaking away, weakening the fog's hold on the land. Murdio watches the final part of the town become free of fog, revealing the shell of civilization. The light returns to Murdio.

"That was fast," says Murdio as he watches the light begin to sink down a bit.

"Yes, well because we aren't higher ranking angels we have a limit to our power," the voice explains.

"True, however, even the smallest light has a purpose in this world," Murdio says.

"That's big words from the mighty Murdio," another voice replies, creating a glowing light behind Murdio.

Murdio then watches two more specks of light appear from the stale air.

"Yeah, like, how powerful could you be if you had our power?" another light says, turning Murdio's attention once more.

"Let's go," the last light says, causing the lights to flash themselves through the ruins.

Murdio spins around, alone once again with darkness. He looks at the sky, finding the lone source of light amongst the dark. Rising brightly above him, a red sphere casts a glow over the land. Murdio watches the light burst with brightness, forcing him to look away. The light fades, allowing Murdio to turn back, seeing the light's pure form.

From out of the confines of the speck, an angel reveals itself with scars from the action. Its wings struggle to hold onto the few feathers remaining, his clothes torn.

"What is your name?" Murdio asks, watching the being look down at its new form.

"Feronis, Sir," Feronis says, beginning to look around at the broken buildings around them.

"What's wrong?" Murdio asks.

"Guardian angels rarely take form within such a demonic place," Feronis replies, folding his wings across his chest

"Why is that?" Murdio asks.

"We are able to repel the evil with our light more than with our bodies," Feronis says, sending his wings behind him.

"Tell me, have you seen a golden light shoot through the sky into this place?" Murdio asks.

"You mean the object that beast had in his possession?" Feronis asks tersely.

Before Murdio answers, a chill fills the air, a fierce wind whipping around them. "Where is he?" Murdio demands, trying to be heard over the screaming wind.

"I'm here," a voice says. From out of the barreling winds, a bolt of lightning drops from the sky, wrapping itself around Feronis's leg.

Feronis attempts to return to his light form as it wraps tightly around him. Before Murdio can move, Feronis screams as the lightning throws him violently into the sides of one of the buildings nearby.

The cry gets fainter and Murdio watches the imagery begin to drip like water, revealing it to be nothing more than a facade. All over, Murdio watches the reveal before his eyes, uncovering a much darker landscape. Before the darkness can settle into the sand, an enormous shadow takes control over the red glow. Turning his attention to it, Murdio finds an unsettling castle taking up the horizon.

The castle, with stones throughout, remains unstable with demonic energy separating the twisting spires. The massive frame extends the entire length of the ruins, allowing no light to shine down upon its ground. A sudden, muffled scream forces Murdio to break his stare. From out of a tower, a skeleton appears with a string of light, dropping down into a cocoon of light.

"Feronis!" Murdio gasps.

He listens as the scream disappears as they go inside another tower. Murdio starts toward the main entrance, the way appearing to be clear. As he gets closer, he takes in the size of the building before going through the doorway. He stops as something within the door catches his attention.

Murdio finds himself in the center of two skeletons patrolling without a means of escape. He turns back, reaching his hand through the opening to try to escape, the flesh from his hand suddenly disintegrating. Seeing them getting closer, Murdio breathes in and steps through. Once on the other side, he hides behind a nearby wall as their footsteps grow louder. Remaining silent, Murdio looks around the corner just as the two skeleton guards make their way around.

Before he can do anything, the two split up, turning away from his location. Exhaling, Murdio drops his head before reopening his eyes, taking in his surroundings. Shelves are plastered all across the room, except for an open doorway. As he continues to examine the area, Murdio jumps back, finding a shadow crawling across the floor.

Murdio charges out the door, unwilling to wait around to see the source. Once out of view, Murdio puts his back against the wall, peeking back into the room. Inside, the shadows come to a stop before breaking into smaller ones, spreading through the room. From the other side of the trembling wall, two skeletons behind robes appear, dragging a rusty chain behind them. At the other end of the chain, Feronis remains unconscious as they approach the doorway next to Murdio.

"Master wants him in there," one of the skeletons says.

"Sounds good to me," the other skeleton replies, making his way to Feronis's shifting body. His arms underneath Feronis's body, the skeleton lifts him and then turns to the door.

Before it can make its way inside, Murdio finds a place to hide within the darkness. He watches it throw Feronis's limp body onto the stone floor in the center of the room. Once his body goes still, the two unwrap the chain from between their bones, tossing it into the room next to Feronis.

"Now be good," the skeleton chuckles, walking back outside.

Murdio remains in the shadows, examining the fresh wounds on Feronis's mortal body. Before he can move a muscle, his eyes catch the shadow of the skeletons beyond the doorway.

"Just to make sure nothing happens to you," one of the skeletons says. Its hand infuses with a shapeless shadow, taking the form of a hand. It then raises its hand to one of the corners, releasing dark matter, suffocating the space between them.

After a couple of seconds, Murdio gingerly makes his way over to Feronis's body. "Feronis, are you alive?" Murdio whispers.

After a moment, Feronis lets out a painful groan, struggling to grasp for air. Realizing he is trapped, Feronis struggles weakly to break free from the chain. "Murdio is that you?" Feronis asks.

"Yes, it's me, now how I can get you out of those unholy chains?" Murdio asks, inspecting the chains.

"There is only one way to break them," a voice says.

Murdio and Feronis freeze, searching for the source when suddenly out of the wall a being appears, hidden behind a flowing cloak. It then lowers its hood, revealing a familiar angel.

"Chalima!" Murdio gasps. "How can I break the chains?"

Chalima walks past him, kneeling beside Feronis, placing her hand upon the glowing shackles.

"You can do nothing," Chalima says after a moment.

"So then how can he break free if there is no way," Murdio demands.

Chalima shakes her head, placing her hands above the chains continuing to release traces of demonic energy.

"You can't, but he can," Chalima says, turning back to Feronis who quickly looks at her.

"I don't have the power to do something like that," Feronis says doubtfully.

"Like this," Chalima says, lifting her hands further up his chest. Before he can speak, Chalima punctures Feronis's chest with her hand. Feronis screams as Chalima pulls back the skin and bone of his chest, revealing the beating heart inside of his ribcage.

"What have you done?" Murdio asks, rushing over to Feronis's side.

"Showing you the gateway to free him," Chalima says, pointing down at his heart.

"All I see is his heart," Murdio replies.

"That's because you don't see the real image," Chalima says, placing her hand over the heart.

Murdio watches the heart change color and shape, allowing darkness to intrude into the heart's chambers. "How does that answer my question?" Murdio asks, continuing to stare at Feronis's open chest.

"He must rid himself of all the negativity," Chalima says, returning his chest back to normal. Both Murdio and Chalima nod, even as Feronis stares blankly at their faces.

"How do I do that?" Feronis asks.

"I will show you," Murdio says, looking back at him. Murdio then looks at Chalima whose hand reaches back, pulling out a bronze spear with an indentation from handle to blade.

Chalima then places it flat in her hands, handing it over to Murdio.

The moment Murdio grabs it, a light begins to rise from the spear, spreading into the darkness filling the room.

"What is that?" Feronis asks, nervously.

"The spear of Lazarin. It can free any heart from darkness," Chalima says, stepping away.

"I need to strike it directly into your heart," Murdio says, banging suddenly echoing in the room.

"Quit your struggling," a voice yells out as the doorknob twists. The twisting ceases, allowing things to return to normal.

"You have got to be kidding me," Feronis says, beginning to violently shake in one last attempt to break free.

"I am serious," Murdio says, pointing the sharp edge between the rows of chain around Feronis's chest.

Chalima kneels behind Feronis, holding him still, preventing any further movement.

"Do you want to be free?" Chalima asks, looking down at Feronis.

"I do," Feronis says, staring up at the spear. His eyes shut as Murdio lowers the spear, striking the top layer of Feronis's chest. Starting in the tip, light begins to burst out, causing his skin to glow. Feeling a sensation, Feronis opens his eyes, looking down at the rippling skin around the spear.

Murdio lifts the spear away, leaving the light spreading inside his chest. Feronis's limbs beginning to glow, the chains dissipating into dust. Once free, the light sinks back into the depths of his chest, when suddenly the sound of steps turns their attention to the shadows. Before their eyes, a single figure appears, blazing behind a dark robe except for a glowing cross in the center of his chest.

"Who are you?" asks Feronis, feeling Chalima release him.

"Your Father!" a voice bellows out, causing Murdio to lower the spear down to his side. The figure fades, leaving the cross hanging in the air. It then levitates to Feronis. Before he can move, the cross passes through him.

"What is this new figure?" Murdio asks, looking over at Feronis as he places his hands on his bare chest.

"I can answer that for you," a voice says.

"Enlighten me," Murdio says, turning his attention throughout the room.

After a couple seconds, Murdio turns his head when he feels a weight press upon his body. Murdio looks to Feronis and Chalima, seeing them struggling to move. A rumbling catches their attention as waves of energy start to send ripples down each wall. A massive cloud starts to seep into the chamber, eventually filling the emptiness. As the seconds pass, the cloud darkens the room, making it impossible to see. After a few seconds, light bursts through the cloud, returning sight back to them. As the cloud dissipates, they find their surroundings no longer dark and dismal. The walls no longer exist, leaving them in the shadows of Heaven's main gate. They continue, beginning to feel a weight being taken from their bodies.

"I sincerely hope this answers your questions, my children," a voice bellows out. The gates spread wide, revealing to the three God himself. They drop to a knee as God approaches, the gate closing behind Him.

"Why have you brought us here?" Murdio asks, lifting his head to see

God coming toward them.

"I can answer that, but first, rise my children," God replies, allowing them to stand up from the ground.

"Something in your possession needs to be brought here in haste," God replies, extending His hand to Murdio.

Murdio looks down to find the spear lifting itself from out of his possession.

"You mean this was given to aid me," Feronis says, placing his hands upon his heart. While they look on, Murdio grabs the spear from the air, bringing it inches away from God's fingertips. Hesitantly, Murdio watches as God grabs hold of the spear, taking it into His hand.

"That saved me," Feronis says, watching God bringing the spear closer to His body.

"Yes, and now it should return here to wait for its rightful owner," God says when two angels drop from the sky.

"Per your request, we have come to be of service," they say, bowing.

God nods, approaching them with the spear in hand. He then gives them each a side of it, causing them to look down upon the weapon. "Put this somewhere safe, out of reach of any demon," God says in a serious tone.

The two grip the spear firmly, looking up at God. "We shall place this where nothing can take possession of it."

"Afterwards, return to the battlefield with your fellow angels," God says.

The two take their leave, heading deep into the blue sky leaving Murdio, Feronis, and Chalima with God. Once out of sight, God turns his attention to the three, catching Feronis still looking into the sky. "You may go with them."

"Are you certain?" asks Feronis, looking back to the sky.

"Just know there is no tranquility in their final destination," God says.

"I understand, and I am ready for whatever it may have in store," Feronis says, wings extending outward. Feronis then turns to Murdio and Chalima.

Murdio steps toward him, placing a hand upon one of his shoulders.

"May you deliver vengeance in the name of the Father."

Feronis places his own hand on top of Murdio's. "Thank you, Murdio, may you find divinity in that world." Feronis then turns his attention to Chalima.

"No need," Chalima says with a wave of her hand and a smile.

"What?" Feronis asks in wonder, turning to God.

"Chalima will be going with you," says God, allowing Feronis to turn back to Chalima.

"I must deliver sentencing, for the enemy lacks repentance," Chalima says, looking down at the mace hanging from her side.

"Well then let us take our leave," Feronis says, watching Chalima lift into the air.

"Yes, just do me a favor Feronis," Chalima says teasingly.

"What is it?" Feronis asks.

"Try to keep up with me," Chalima says, taking off into the sky.

Feronis quickly rises, propelling himself upwards as he starts to head off behind Chalima. As they vanish from sight, God and Murdio face each other, stoic without an angel in sight.

"What am I to do next?" Murdio asks.

"You must complete your mission," God says.

"I must recover the staff you have given me before locating the halo," Murdio says, kneeling in front of God.

"Indeed, and only then will you return amongst us," God says, placing His hand on Murdio's shoulder. "I do have one last thing to assist you." Before Murdio's eyes, God forms another staff inside his hand. God extends it to Murdio, who takes hold of the weapon.

"What is this for?" Murdio asks, staring at the weapon.

"To assist you temporarily against the demonic duo," God says.

Murdio rises back up to his feet, placing the staff along his back. He breathes deeply, feeling a new confidence to aid him in the darkness. "Amen."

God moves His hand, placing His palm against Murdio's forehead. At His touch, Murdio falls through the cloudy surface out of Heaven and God's view.

CHAPTER SEVEN
Battling the Demons

MURDIO OPENS HIS EYES, finding himself back on the sandy ground. After a breath, Murdio finds his bearing, seeing the demonic castle. He finds no sign of the skeletons that dwell inside. He cautiously approaches the castle as the wind whistles through the walkways. Inside, Murdio looks for any presence of the skeletons patrolling about. To his surprise, however, the halls remain empty with only the sounds of his own breathing accompanying him.

As he makes his way down the halls, he cautiously looks around, the emptiness becoming monotonous. He passes into a secondary room, where bones have turned into dust, the dust coating the walls. On top of a bone pile, a broken skull sits, missing its lower jaw. Murdio approaches the cinder pile, a diabolical laugh suddenly catching his attention, echoing down a winding staircase. Walking over to the stairs, Murdio stops at the first step, noticing a trail of burnt footprints on the steps.

"I'm coming," he says, readying himself for whatever awaits him.

With each step, the chuckling grows louder, until he arrives at the top, where he finds a single door. Murdio reaches for the door when a deafening scream roars through the cracks. Stepping back, Murdio covers his ears until the scream turns to silence.

Carefully, Murdio places his ear against the door, placing his hand on the doorknob. With a turn, Murdio opens the door gingerly, breathing in the stale air of the darkness outside. In front of him, a large castle wall sits in the distance, a single opening facing his direction. Faint rumbling comes from below and Murdio looks in time to watch blocks of bones connect themselves, forming a path.

Once the last one is secure, Murdio hesitantly places a foot down on the walkway. Before he can take another step, the wind carries another round of laughter. After a couple of steps, Murdio stops to look at his destination awaiting him.

"No turning back now, Murdio," a voice calls, causing the door to slam shut behind Murdio.

The walkway rattles violently, nearly shaking Murdio off, causing the blocks behind him to crash to the ground. Once the movement ceases, Murdio turns back to the opening, struggling to regain his composure. The bridge sways with the swirling winds, forcing Murdio to slowly make his way forward. With each step, Murdio makes his way toward the next tower and the solid flooring waiting for him.

Looking back, Murdio is surprised to find the first tower not as far as he thought before turning his attention back to the open doorway. Murdio takes a deep breath, the opening now only a step away. After he shakes away the confusion, Murdio takes the massive step onto the tower's platform. Once more, Murdio looks back at the opposite tower as the remaining blocks crash to the ground.

"Another step closer," Murdio whispers to himself, watching the pathway ahead of him.

As Murdio steps into a dimly lit hallway once more, he finds two branching hallways, each with a door at the end. On one side, Murdio finds a shining light trying to escape through the cracks and splinters on the door. On the other, just a plain door.

He steps to the plain one first, swinging the door open. A candlelit pedestal stands on each side of the doorway with a dirty, cobweb-covered shelf in the middle. Murdio turns back and forth, thoughts beginning to fill his mind about the ongoing war growing all around him. Murdio looks at the shining door, feeling a compulsion to proceed.

Approaching the door, Murdio's hand convulses as he reaches for the ashy doorknob. With a deep breath, he grabs it, knocking off some of the ash, revealing gold underneath the layers of ash. Murdio continues to turn the knob as the door creaks, revealing more of the light. Bit by bit the light escapes the door, showing more of what is waiting on the other side.

Just as the door fully opens, a massive explosion of light startles Murdio, suffocating the darkness behind him. Murdio makes his way into it, his eyes adjusting to the brightness as it starts to dim. As he continues forward, he struggles to see through the white haze. To his surprise, behind the light beholds the Heaven he knew except there was no peace or tranquility. Murdio feels his heart drop as he watches the battle between the Fallen skeletal army versus the Angels of Heaven.

Neither side make any dent in the opposition and Murdio finds himself witness to a never-ending battle if things remain the same. Murdio grabs hold of the doorframe, debating if he should step onto the battlefield. He surprises himself when he suddenly steps back, slamming the door shut, causing the coating of dust to slide down the door. To his surprise, the ash reveals scribbling text on the wall.

"Chaos," Murdio whispers, deciphering the wording on the door.

Murdio turns away, walking back to the first door, finding it still open. He stares momentarily into the pitch-black waiting for him beyond the candlelight. Before walking through, Murdio pauses and takes one last look at the second door. Shockingly, Murdio sees nothing but a stone wall in place of the door.

He makes his way through the dark opening, finding himself in a massive room with torches all over. He makes his way into the center of the chamber, trying to make out his surroundings.

Heavy stomping suddenly causes the floor beneath his feet to tremble. Murdio turns quickly, finding two flaming spheres appearing out of the shadows on the opposite side. Each passing moment, the glow from the fire grows in strength before Murdio's eyes.

"I see you made it. It's just too bad you have to die," a voice says, delivering another chuckle.

Struggling to make the source out, Murdio watches an enormous shadow, darker than the rest, step forward. Unable to make it out, the shadow charges at Murdio, gaining strength from the shadows cast by the pillars between them. Before Murdio can dodge the beast, it reappears in front of him, knocking him down to the ground. Behind a plume of ash, Murdio struggles to get back to his feet. As Murdio gets to his feet, he looks over at the creature, watching it leap onto the wall. The creature disappears into the darkness, suddenly returning to the shadows behind the two blazing orbs. The chuckle rings out once more, echoing through the emptiness inside the room.

"Stop hiding, Velkaun!" Murdio yells, looking around the room.

"You angels are never fun," a voice mocks, causing the torches on the next level to light one by one. Approaching the farthest corner, the torches stop lighting, allowing the darkness to remain in place.

"Typical demonic cowardice," Murdio says, trying to make out any sort of figure within the darkness.

"If the angel says light it up, then I best comply with its wishes," Velkaun says.

Murdio watches the last few torches light, revealing Lukas, a fire burning around his hands.

"You look confused," Lukas says, lifting his hands up before blowing them out.

"I think he is," Velkaun says, stepping out from the darkness inside the hall, a ball of flames attached to a chain in each hand. They both start to move toward him, passing through the shadows along the walls.

"Do I sense a bit of excitement to see me?" Lukas asks, turning to Velkaun. With each step, Lukas leaves another burning footstep into the stones.

"Not in the least," Velkaun replies, extending his hand out for Lukas who extends a hand back. Their hands come together, causing an eruption which releases a bone-rattling wave throughout the room.

"Not to destroy this unholy moment, but I am here for the staff and the halo," Murdio says, turning to the demonic brothers.

"Excuse me, but I'm going to take care of this pest," Velkaun says, releasing Lukas's hand when he makes his way over to Murdio.

"Bring it on," Murdio says, taking the staff off his back and holding it across his chest. Murdio watches as Velkaun stalks closer, his black eyes and a dangerously evil grin trying to break Murdio's confidence.

"This will definitely be an entertaining battle," Lukas says, easing onto a throne of fire made by nearby torches.

Murdio watches Velkaun, knowing he is waiting for Murdio to make the first move. With a twirl of his staff, Murdio charges forward.

"You have just made a foolish mistake," Velkaun says, disappearing back into the shadows, causing Murdio to stop in his tracks.

Lukas sits up as the darkness begins to ripple and quake. As both Murdio and Lukas look on in suspense, a pair of three-pronged claws rip through the darkness. Murdio's eyes widen, watching as piece by piece Velkaun's new form breaks from its demonic cocoon. The enormous creature steps from the shadow, shaking the floor with each step.

Murdio stares in fear, retreating a couple of steps as the creature continues forward. He looks at a creature, taking in its stone-like physique, even as darkness continues to corrupt the surface.

"Murdio, I want you to meet Velkaun the Golem," Lukas says, sitting back in his throne as fire swirls from the armrests.

Velkaun towers over Murdio, eyes suffocating in darkness and claws dripping hate.

"I shall vanquish you," Murdio says. Velkaun moves much faster than he expected and before Murdio can locate him, a claw sends Murdio crashing into the bone pile.

"Out of pity, I shall even the odds," Lukas replies, watching Murdio stand above the bones. Lukas reaches inside the fire, pulling out the half of the staff which catches Murdio's attention. Gleaming, Lukas drops it onto the ground just outside of his reach.

"How dare you help a spawn of God!" Velkaun roars angrily, looking at Murdio stumbling to his feet.

"I am merely making this fight more interesting," Lukas says.

"It's powerless without the other half," Velkaun growls. He reaches back, sending his claw forward through the broken pillars.

Murdio manages to dodge the monstrous claw, watching it lodge inside the wall. As Velkaun struggles to free himself, Lukas watches in disbelief from his throne. Before his eyes, Velkaun pulls it free, pebbles scattering throughout.

Velkaun turn back to see Murdio kneeling, staff in hand. Velkaun takes another swing, Murdio catching a glimpse from the shadows. Before the strike lands, Lukas erupts from the throne onto the next level using his flames. Safe out of the way, Lukas watches Velkaun's claw shred through the throne, burning it on impact.

Seeing the throne a molten pile of rubble, Lukas turns his attention to Velkaun. "Next time how about you aim for your target."

"It's not my fault that your puny throne was in my path," Velkaun roars.

"Fine, but would you mind telling me where your toy has gone to?" Lukas demands, pointing over to the pile of bones.

"Where did he go?" Velkaun asks, looking around the room.

"No idea, I'm just going to watch you do your thing from here," Lukas says, perching himself against a wall.

"Good, so let me finish this," Velkaun roars, crashing through another pillar.

"Per your request, my demonic brother," Lukas says, resting against the wall between a set of lit torches.

"Come on out," Velkaun roars, whipping his tongue back and forth.

"Oh, but who is hiding?" Murdio asks, causing Velkaun search for him throughout the room.

Velkaun stops, turning his attention upward to the fracturing stones making up the ceiling.

Lukas stands up when Velkaun turns his back, revealing Murdio perching himself among the stones on his back. Just as Lukas is about to speak, Murdio turns, firing the staff into the wall inches from his head. He then turns his attention to the other half of the staff, lodged among the shards of rocks along Velkaun's back. Before he can reach his hand out for it, Murdio holds on tightly as Velkaun beginning to charge.

Unable to escape, Velkaun crashes into the wall, rattling the stone frame beneath Murdio's feet. As Murdio struggles to keep his balance, Velkaun launches himself once again. Crevices begin to appear as cracks spread, forcing Murdio to jump, managing to grab hold of a broken ledge connecting to the second floor. Murdio lifts himself onto stable ground, Velkaun reappearing from out of the shadows.

Velkaun slams his hands into the ground, causing a quake to spread around the room.

Murdio watches as a wave of ash moves forward and he slides quickly behind one of the remaining pillars left standing. Once things calm, Murdio releases a deep breath, stepping out from hiding.

"You pest, it is time to die," Velkaun roars. Velkaun opens his mouth, creating a foul creation from within the depths of his bowels. It swells within his jaws until Velkaun is unable to contain the darkness. In a single breath, the nightmarish creation explodes, and Murdio drops to the ground watching as the bones disintegrate around him.

Before the screams can take hold, Murdio scrambles inside a hollow crevice just as the room darkens. Bracing himself, the blast vibrates the landscape, causing Murdio to cover his ears. After the final scream fades, the atmosphere calms allowing Murdio to relax his tense muscles.

"I think you got him," Lukas calls from above.

After listening for any sound, Velkaun roars, his body dissolves into the shadows. Once the last shadow disappears, Velkaun appears in his normal state. He sneers, kneeling as his hand wraps around the other half of the staff. Once it is firmly in his grasp, Velkaun stands back up returning to his search.

"Well I guess we don't need this anymore," Velkaun says, launching the broken piece into a mound of debris.

"That was easier than I thought it," Lukas says, pulling the other half from out of the wall. He jumps down to the main floor, Velkaun smirking as the eerie silence returns to the room.

Out of their sight, Murdio reopens his eyes, seeing the blank material of the wall, hearing the faintest of footsteps outside. Struggling to make little noise, Murdio turns to the sliver of light outside when he spots them. Lukas walks over to Velkaun, holding the other half of the staff. Once they are together, Lukas launches the other half at the other side of debris pile.

Murdio wipes his eyes when the gleaming halves catch his sight inches from his grasp. The color in his eyes dissipates, watching as the two halves merge together into a single form. Murdio extends his arm, grabbing hold of the staff, a rejuvenating power fusing within his body. The light starts to fade, restoring Murdio's strength, unbeknownst to the demonic brothers.

"Now it is my turn." Murdio steps out from the opening as the two search for any sign of him. After stepping to the edge of the second level, Murdio enters their sight, causing them to freeze in disbelief.

"Seems you lost your touch," Lukas comments.

"It appears this one is fortunate," Velkaun replies at the same time.

Murdio drops to the main floor with his staff in hand, causing the ground to crumble around him.

"Well, Brother, this is your fight and yours alone," Lukas says, a vortex of flames appearing from the throne rubble. Lukas then steps within the swirling blaze, vanishing before their eyes. It spins out, leaving Velkaun and Murdio staring at each other.

"Let me show you an actual instrument of destruction," Velkaun says, lifting his hand up into the air.

Murdio watches shadows swirl from around Velkaun's arm leading up to his hand. The shadows take shape, manifesting into a trident over Velkaun's palm. Around the handle, darkness circles, forcing spikes to protrude from within the shadows. Unwilling to wait any longer, Murdio charges him, staff spinning dangerously in the dense air.

Before the staff can come within a hair's breadth, Velkaun slides out of the way, delivering an uppercut, sending Murdio stumbling backward. Velkaun stalks his way over, watching Murdio drop to a knee. Watching Murdio struggle to regain himself, Velkaun approaches from behind, lifting the trident high into the air. Then with all his might, Velkaun unleashes the trident downward.

Before Velkaun can drive the trident any further, Murdio twirls, spearing Velkaun into the wall with his staff. Velkaun's back slams hard against it, allowing Murdio to lift him up. He steps back before driving Velkaun once more into the unforgiving wall. Struggling to breathe, Velkaun looks at Murdio, watching him take a step away when he charges at him. Before the staff can pierce his chest, Velkaun steps back, fading into the shadows on the wall.

Murdio stops, finding no trace of his presence. He slams his hands into the stone, causing them to bend around his fists.

Meanwhile, from out of the wall behind him, Velkaun reemerges from the opposite end. "I'm not so easily defeated." With a grin, Velkaun shakily places the trident inside his hand as he looks over at an unsuspecting Murdio. With a roar, Velkaun charges, slashing his trident through the stone pillars.

Hearing the thunderous rumbling, Murdio crouches, just in time to block Velkaun's strike. The room quakes as each of their attacks counters the others' force. Murdio counters with a swing around only to have Velkaun's trident deflect it. Feeling the vibration in his hands, Murdio kicks Velkaun back into a pillar before attempting another strike. Before he can land another hit, Velkaun dodges the blow.

As Murdio struggles to recover, Velkaun thrusts the trident, catching Murdio's attention. Murdio spins away, causing the trident to miss as he prepares another strike. Murdio charges forward only to watch Velkaun slip away, shoving him into the ground. With an exhale shooting dust into the air, Murdio jumps back up, hands firmly around the handle of his staff. Both struggle to catch their breath before charging at one another with their weapons high in the air. They clash with equal strength, Murdio's staff falling between two of the points on the trident.

"Just give up," Velkaun roars, trying to push the trident forward. Finding no give, Velkaun and Murdio remain at a stalemate while Lukas looks on.

Murdio smirks, managing to maintain his strength when Velkaun lifts his foot and aims it at Murdio's leg. Weakening his base, Murdio lowers the weapon, allowing Velkaun to pull the trident back before unloading another strike. Just as the trident gets close, Murdio manages to duck out of the way and spins around.

Unable to defend it, Velkaun watches him turn around with the staff aimed lower. The sweep takes him off his feet, causing his body to turn upside down. Velkaun smashes into the ground in front of Murdio, the trident falling innocently to the floor.

"I don't give up," Murdio says, slamming the staff into Velkaun's back causing his body to deepen the indentation beneath him.

Murdio then shakes his head, kneeling to grab hold of Velkaun as he barely clings to consciousness. He lifts Velkaun to his feet, and Velkaun laughs hysterically when demonic energy begins to seep from Velkaun's pores. Murdio steps back, watching the energy swirl into a puddle around both their feet. He watches his feet disappear into the darkness, feeling them sink beneath the ground. Attempting to struggle to break free, Velkaun launches himself, grabbing hold of Murdio. Before he can move, Velkaun falls beneath the energy, bringing Murdio with him and out of Lukas's sight.

Beneath the surface, a world of darkness and spirits surround them as they crash land on the unstable ground. Murdio struggles to take in the surroundings before turning to see Velkaun dusting himself off. He backs away as two demons crawl from the darkness and ensnare Murdio's limbs.

With Murdio helpless, Velkaun unwraps the line of spikes from his trident before making his way forward. He steps behind Murdio, throwing a chain over Murdio's head. He then pulls it back, tightly wrapping it around Murdio's neck. Squeezing the air from his lungs, Velkaun grabs both ends with one hand, freeing the other. As he holds the chain with one hand, Velkaun turns back, using his other hand to rip a seam within the demon world. With the hole widening, Velkaun, along with the demonic shadows, throw Murdio inside of the crevice.

Murdio crashes down onto the roof of the castle, the portal remaining open in the air above him. With Murdio prone on the ground, Velkaun jumps out of the opening, which closes behind him in a flash of lightning. Just as Velkaun lands, the chain of spikes resurfaces around the trident's base. Velkaun stalks his way toward Murdio, his weapon hanging to the side, dripping darkness.

"Your father can't help you here," Velkaun sneers.

He watches Murdio choke down some air, his hands grasping at where the chain had been around his neck. As Velkaun steps closer, Murdio manages to get to his knees, wiping the blood from his mouth. After releasing a massive snarl, Velkaun draws back the trident as Murdio grabs his staff, defending the blow. Velkaun angrily slams his trident repeatedly, Murdio struggling to keep the weapon away. Out of frustration, Velkaun lays his weight on top of the trident trying to lessen the distance. When he doesn't succeed, Murdio flips Velkaun over his head, keeping both hands on the staff. Velkaun tumbles on the ground, allowing Murdio to lift himself from the stones.

After nearly falling off the castle's roof, Velkaun stands on the edge of the building, looking back over to Murdio.

"No one can save you from me either," Murdio says confidently as once again the two charge each other. This time, however, Murdio delivers a blow to Velkaun's side before sliding underneath the swinging trident. With Velkaun unable to stop his momentum, Murdio punches Velkaun in the back of the head, sending him stumbling to his knees.

Velkaun then turns his head, struggling to get back to his feet. As he gets up, Velkaun rushes with the trident to his side. The trident strikes Murdio, sending him flying into one of the posts protruding from out of the corner of the roof. Before Murdio can stand up, the post collapses down to the bottom level.

Murdio looks at Velkaun, his hand tightening around the center of the staff. The staff brightens around his hand when lightning chains itself around the staff's golden metal. Once the crackling bolt wraps around completely, the staff unleashes a bolt of electricity into Velkaun's direction.

Velkaun's eyes roll back, allowing demonic energy to infiltrate the base of the trident. Then, from out of the three tips, screaming blasts screech their way toward the bolt of light. In a collision, a massive explosion ricochets into silence, sending both Murdio and Velkaun sliding back to their respective sides. Both their hands continuing to glow, the two remain silent even as the clouds above grow violently. With the first crack of lightning from above, Murdio and Velkaun rush to one another, their weapons ready to attack.

Able to dodge Velkaun's swing, Murdio sends his staff twisting around Velkaun's midsection. After a couple more blows, Murdio drops Velkaun to his knees, struggling to take in a single breath. Then, as he attempts another shot, he shifts the staff around, turning the blunt end into Velkaun's forehead.

Velkaun crashes to the ground eyes shut, leaving Murdio to make his way over to the body. Before he can make a move, the ground rumbles behind Murdio when stones shoot upwards, revealing a skeletal figure. Murdio turns around, watching the skeleton secure itself to the ground. Reaching for his staff, Murdio watches as a single vortex erupts through the roof. The skeleton dissolves within the swirling blaze, the vortex unravelling into the sky.

Murdio returns his attention to the barely conscious Velkaun before looking to the gaping hole feet away.

As he kneels down, Velkaun opens his eyes, grabbing a tight hold of Murdio's chest dragging him once again through another portal. Lying in the land of shadows, the two remain still as reddish eyes appear all around them. Before Murdio can raise his staff, Velkaun thrusts the trident into Murdio's ribs, causing him to fall weakly. Attempting to reach back, Velkaun delivers a punch to the back of Murdio's head.

With an evil laugh, Velkaun tears open a portal back to the world just above the gaping hole in the castle's roof. Velkaun then turns to Murdio, seeing him holding his hand on the open wound on the side of his body. Velkaun makes his way toward Murdio as blood starts to seep between his fingers.

"Well, the mighty son of God bleeds like a human." Velkaun kneels down and grabs hold of Murdio, causing him to shift his weight onto his back. A trail of blood follows him as Velkaun drags Murdio's body closer to the opening. Velkaun then throws the trident through the portal using his free hand to pick up Murdio's body.

As Velkaun pauses to watch the stream of blood coming from Murdio's side, Murdio regains some semblance of mind. Trying to shake the cobwebs free, Murdio slams the staff in the center of Velkaun's chest. The impact sends Velkaun falling through the portal, Murdio in tow. The staff strikes Velkaun, and a single lightning bolt enters the staff before exploding within Velkaun's body.

Just as Murdio lands on the new rooftop, Velkaun's body begins to seize before falling through the hole in the roof. As Velkaun gurgles a scream, his body goes limp, smashing into the floor.

Breathing a haggard sigh, Murdio looks at the blood from his wound staining his hands and the ground around him. Murdio then turns his attention back to the darkening crater that holds Velkaun's motionless body.

Velkaun's eyes shut as the trident on the opposite end of the hole begins to dissipate into the pitch black sky. Once shut, they erupt open unleashing a horrifying scream with it.

Murdio turns to see a ball of light explode from out of the crater, casting a glow upon the surroundings. Darkness swallows up the light and unleashes tormenting howls, beginning its trek to the hole in the roof. Murdio spins away, dropping to safety as the demonic darkness continues to expand.

Once the final scream leaves the chamber, Murdio looks back to the now quiet sky before making his way over to the hole. To Murdio's surprise, he finds nothing beyond the broken remains of the chamber below. After a silent moment, Murdio gets to his feet, looking around for any way to get back in.

"To you, he was a demon, but to me, he was a brother," a voice echo.

CHAPTER EIGHT
Defense and Honor

MURDIO WATCHES AS, FROM out of the darkness, flames begin to channel through the air towards him. They land on the other end of the roof before dispersing into falling embers. From out of the remains, Lukas steps through the falling ash. As he steps into view, Murdio catches sight of a golden ring inside his left hand.

"You shall be delivered the same fate," Murdio replies.

Lukas silently looks down upon the glowing halo at his side. "Why would this worthless trinket mean so much to you?" Lukas asks, bouncing the glimmering halo between his hands.

"Let me have it and I'll show you," Murdio says dangerously.

Lukas lifts the halo over his shoulder and pulls back as if to toss the halo to Murdio. Murdio's hands clench when Lukas stops his movements just shy of tossing it to him. "Wow, you actually thought I was just going to give you this halo," Lukas chuckles, a wall of flames appearing between them.

Before long, it disappears, along with Lukas who is nowhere to be found.

"I'm down here," Lukas taunts, waving his hand.

Murdio walks up to the hole to find Lukas standing tall, halo in hand. Without a reply, Murdio jumps down, swinging his staff, forcing Lukas to roll out of the way.

Lukas then looks down when suddenly Murdio catches sight of something on the ground near his feet.

"You have made this too easy for me," Murdio says, reaching to pick up the halo off the ground.

"Look again," Lukas sneers.

Murdio wraps his hand around the faintly glowing halo. Lifting it to his chest, the halo disintegrates into ash, slipping between Murdio's fingers. Enraged, Murdio throws down the remainder before looking to see the grin on Lukas's face. Murdio quickly finds the halo as it reappears in the palm of Lukas's hand. "You shall pay for such an atrocity!"

A flame overcomes the corneas in Lukas's eyes as he smiles at Murdio. "Catch me if you can." He then looks upward as flames swirl around him from the ground below.

Murdio watches on as the fiery vortex curves itself into the direction of the passageway from where Murdio came from. As the wind forces Murdio to grab hold of a pillar, suddenly the vortex explodes through the doorway out into the hallway. While Murdio looks on, struggling to keep hold, the vortex bends around the curve and then disappears.

Murdio chases after the moving vortex, hoping to find Lukas. After the vortex comes to a turn, Murdio freezes in his tracks, finding a wall standing before him.

"Come out demon, wherever you are!"

The bricks suddenly shift, revealing the door labeled 'Matter' from the darkness. As Murdio looks up, the roof splits in half, allowing the vortex to land in front of it. It disperses, leaving a molten figure blocking the entire doorframe. The being stands still, dripping melting stone onto the ground. Murdio watches as the figure grows two massive wings from its back that reach the length of the hallway. Flames continue to burst across its unstable frame and Murdio tightens his grip on his staff as he looks up into its coal eyes.

The monster takes a step, burning a footprint into the stone floor. As Murdio stares at it, it drives a hand deep into its chest, sparks showering around it. When its hand reappears Murdio sees his halo caught between the burning marrow of its fingers. Its eyes pin Murdio as it lifts the halo above its head. It places the halo above its head, letting go as it solidifies into place. Unleashing a horrific scream, the halo erupts into flames, hardening the monster's body.

"Say hello to the real face of all the nightmares!" Lukas bellows as flames spurt from his lips.

"I don't fear you," Murdio replies, readjusting his grip upon the staff.

"Let me break your ignorance," Lukas says, his face solidifying into a single mass, his ashy complexion becoming one piece as fire carves lines across his skin.

Before Murdio can take a step toward him, growling echoes off the walls behind him. Murdio turns, seeing two skeletons lumbering their way inside, Lukas' fire burning away the remnants of their flesh.

"If you think they will stop me then you are mistaken," Murdio says, watching as his words fall on deaf ears.

"They are merely to weaken you," Lukas says, turning around to the door. He grabs hold of the doorknob, causing his crackling bones to sizzle. As the thin metal melts, Lukas opens the door, revealing the cloudy sky on the other side. Before Murdio can turn his head, Lukas jumps out, shooting across the sky with flames trailing behind him.

Turning from the smoke, Murdio looks toward the creeping skeletons.

"Now this is just like a Fallen to run and hide," he comments to himself, charging down the hallway.

The skeletons quicken their pace as Murdio places both hands directly on the staff's center. As one breaks stride and reaches Murdio first, it attempts to swing a dangling arm in his direction. With ease, Murdio shoves away the arm and slams the staff into the skeleton's ribcage. As Murdio pulls back the staff, he manages to extinguish the remaining flames. Before Murdio can strike again, the room goes dark with a single bright light at the opposite end.

"Now Murdio! You must unleash the deliverance!" a mysterious light calls from the darkness.

"What must I do for victory?" Murdio says, squinting his eyes at the single light.

"You must be willing to relinquish yourself for the better of the spirits around you," the voice echoes.

Before Murdio can reply, the single light disappears before the room returns to normal. "FAITH!" Murdio screams with his hand upon the staff. Murdio unleashes a bellowing scream when he snaps the staff in half.

While the two skeletons look on, the pieces grow into their own weapons within his hands. They attack once again as Murdio rolls away from their strikes. As their arms break against the wall, Murdio picks up the weapons and directs them at the skeletons. Their limbs burning on the floor, the two turn their eyes to Murdio.

Without hesitation, Murdio throws one of his weapons into the back of the skeleton's skull. The force sends it through the wall and into the shadows beyond the room. The flames glow dimly within the shadows when the staff reappears from the opening. It flies through the air and lands back into Murdio's hand.

"These odds are better," Murdio says, seeing the other charging him.

The skeleton twists around when its arms regrow from the empty shoulder sockets. It then swings its arms with little control, forcing Murdio to duck beneath the strikes. Even as the warmth of the flames gets near, Murdio lifts his staff to take the impact.

Unable to break his defense, it opens its mouth, a swirling flame growing within, before erupting on Murdio's hands. Clenching his teeth, Murdio watches the flesh peel away from his bare fingertips.

Murdio angrily looks up at the skeleton, bits of ash stuck to its cheekbones. Murdio's eyes lighten when the flesh and skin from his fingers begin to regrow around the bone. As it attempts a second attack, Murdio removes one of his hands from the staff just before the last piece of skin can form. Murdio reaches through its ribcage and grabs hold of the flames before it can make its way up to the throat.

The skeleton struggles as Murdio manages to keep hold, lifting it off the ground.

Murdio watches as its hands drop as the fire swells within its vertebrae. Each vertebra starts to pucker as the flames inside cause them to glow. The swelling suddenly stops when it reaches just beneath Murdio's hand, which clamps it shut.

With the flames caught, the bones begin to expand as the skeleton struggles to get free. The coal eyes drop out of their sockets, and onto the ground as the skeleton shudders violently.

Murdio then throws the skeleton into the opposing wall, the fire continuing to build inside. The wall shatters causing an explosion which forces the door open. Before turning to the door, Murdio grabs hold of his two staffs.

"You will never make it," the Fallen yells as flames erupt all around its head. Before Murdio can reply, a massive fireball erupts from within it, launching the skull into the room. It passes over Murdio's shoulder, blazing a trail toward the door, where it crashes to the floor.

"I'm coming for you." Murdio jumps out of the darkness and into the open world.

He falls helplessly, plowing through layers of clouds. Beneath him, a lush gray land sits between two sides waging war. Piles of bones are scattered between the corpses of fallen angels. Murdio's eyes widen when the land caves in, opening up to consume him.

The shades of grey fade from view as the landscape twists and bends in every direction. Continuing to fall, Murdio watches as the land crumbles, and demonic terrain rises to the surface. Between the patches of evil, fire erupts, sending plumes of black smoke into the sky. Unable to stop, Murdio helplessly watches as the molten ground keeps the now sky above at bay. Unable to direct his landing, Murdio slams into the ground, sending up a burst of ash and coal.

Lying motionless, Murdio catches his breath between plumes of ash. His vision blurry, Murdio gets a glimpse of his staff by his side. He manages to extend his fingers, grabbing it in his hand. Struggling to take a breath, Murdio looks around beyond the edge of the crater.

The world is dark and barren, the sky twisting with flames, blending the smoke into the black sky. From out of the silence, three shadows appear.

"Are you friend or foe?" Murdio manages, struggling to his feet.

Without a response, Lukas appears, unleashing a clubbing blow, sending Murdio back down. "The term is the executioner." Lukas then steps back, allowing two demons to crawl down into the shallow crater.

They wrap their pointed claws around Murdio's feet and drag him from the crater. They drop him at Lukas's feet as he looks on in disgust, the halo burning over his head.

"Master, how shall we take care of this fallen angel?" one of the demons ask, crawling away from Lukas.

"Let him experience hopelessness," Lukas says.

The demon nods before picking Murdio up, throwing him over his shoulder as wings sprout from his back. After securing him, it flies away leaving the other alone with Lukas.

"Why not kill him where he lay?" the demon asks, causing Lukas to turn his attention to him.

"I have my reasons, which are of no concern to an evil spawn," Lukas snaps, causing the demon to lower its head.

"I'm sorry, my lord," the demon says, keeping its head down to the ground.

"Believe me, I know," Lukas says, manifesting a boulder from the chunks of coal and flames riddling the air. Then with a flick of the wrist, the meteor crashes down, sending pieces of bone all around, destroying his minion. Shaking his head, Lukas spreads his massive wings and lifts off the ground into the darkness above.

Meanwhile, the demon flies with Murdio, barely conscious, his staff slung across it's back. Murdio squints his eyes, finding himself facing the endless terrain of the demonic land.

"You may not be awake, but the master has plans to destroy you," the demon whispers, changing direction to a crumbling ruin in the distance.

As the ground approaches, Murdio lifts the staff, jabbing it into the demon's back. He pushes it hard, forcing the other end out through its ribcage, inches from his own body. With the demon losing control, Murdio manages to slide from his grasp, pulling his staff back out at the same time. Murdio tumbles safely onto a hill while the demon careens through the sky, fire erupting from the wound in its chest.

Murdio stumbles forward, seeing a campsite with skeletons patrolling around it. Making their way up and down the central pathway, they surround prisoner souls, going about their business in the fortress's shadow.

Murdio is frozen as a fireball crashes down between the camp and the monstrous building. Lukas rises from the fiery crater and proceeds through the main entrance into the building.

"I know where I must go," Murdio whispers, looking up at massive walls as pillars of flames shoot from all corners.

Murdio slides down to the wall, forcing the ash above his feet as he comes to a stop. Kicking the ash off, Murdio finds the entranceway bare as a skeleton's bones. He slowly makes his way through the doorway, keeping a lookout even though there were no shadows in sight. He peeks inside to find what may be awaiting him. Inside tents are scattered about, made of bone and skin, as souls gently float along a path. Murdio takes a deep breath and slinks his way just outside the first tent.

After taking a second glance, the souls disappear leaving just the skeletal guards. They begin to gather from all over the camp, collecting single file into a line.

"What are you doing here?" a deep voice says.

Murdio looks back, seeing a twisting soul rise from the ground with glowing red eyes. "I'm looking for my tent," Murdio stutters, hiding his hand clutching the staff.

"Oh, and how did an ordinary soul get a staff like that?" the spirit snaps, causing Murdio to feel a bead of sweat drip down his face.

"I found it in the ash just outside," Murdio says, trying to sneak the staff out of the soul's view.

"Liar," the spirit screams, developing a skeletal structure. It then begins to run at Murdio who turns to run in the other direction. His mind races as he realized guards are blocking every exit.

Suddenly, a fleshy hand snatches Murdio away, returning him to a less chaotic place. Murdio finds himself looking into the dead eyes of a spirit whose arms hang to the ground.

"Keep quiet," the spirit whispers, pointing out a dying shrub nearby.

Murdio runs toward it, disappearing just as a pair of skeletons appear.

"I'm only going to ask once. Where is he, Lian?" the skeleton commands. Meanwhile, the other ravages a nearby tent, sending bones everywhere.

"I thought I heard something about you wanting to join our team," the other skeleton says, stopping his destruction.

"I've never been a team player," Lian replies.

Murdio keeps quiet, staring between two branches and their dying leaves. As the two continue their search, Murdio looks over, finding a tent with a slash through one of the sides. He crawls over and lifts the flap just enough to slide underneath. Once the flap folds back, Murdio looks back in surprise to find the tear open, leaving him vulnerable. He looks around, seeing a tent barely standing nearby.

"I don't see him," the skeleton says, looking through the scraps of debris.

Ignoring their words, Murdio keeps his eyes on the tent when a crash catches his attention. Three shadows suddenly bolt around the inside leaving Murdio hunkering down in the open air.

"He no longer populates this tent," Lian says, causing the skeletons to look back at him.

"Where is he now?" the skeleton demands, slamming his foot into the sand.

Murdio watches on as Lian lifts his hand up to the skeleton's jawbone in a threatening manner. "He is probably on his way to the master's dungeon," Lian says, lowering his hand.

The two skeletons turn to one another, nodding before turning back to Lian. "We will find him ourselves," one snaps before the two skeletons storm away, leaving Lian alone inside the tent.

Murdio backs up as the two skeletons rush past him, disappearing from the campsite. He quickly grabs hold of the staff, lifting it off his back and walking into the center of the camp. Murdio sneaks inside the tent next to Lian when suddenly Lian's tent bursts into flames. The eruption rattles the bone frame, throwing Murdio and the spirit away from the burning tent into a shrub.

Watching the tent ablaze, Lukas suddenly appears, stepping from the roaring flames. He momentarily searches before taking off, leaving swirling black smoke in his wake. While Lukas disappears, the tent crumbles with the sounds of cracking bones.

Murdio rolls from the shrub, glancing at the spirit before following the flames behind Lukas. As the fiery trail disappears, Murdio runs over to the opening of the building. With his staff hanging to his side, Murdio slows as he approaches the edge of the walkway. Just as he gets to it, a chain of bright lights passes over his head. Murdio as it crashes into the remaining tents.

One by one the tents erupt in a blaze, joining Lian's tent. After a brief look, Murdio turns back to the flaming shrine of destruction. He approaches the path of stones as flames blaze along the walls. With each step, Murdio carefully passes piles of bones smoldering around the pathway. Even as molten rock swirls around the various towers, Murdio approaches the opening in an uneasy glow.

As he gets closer to the first building, the heat intensifies as the stones cast a brighter light. Murdio approaches the ledge separating the pathway from the shrine itself. As he steps up on the ledge, his eyes catch sight of Lukas in the center of the main floor. Murdio slowly makes his way inside as the blazing demon stands on the ground facing the back side of the shrine so that he can't see Murdio.

"Give me the Halo," Murdio says, slamming the staff into the molten rock. He watches Lukas remain still without a reply, his body suddenly starting to pulse and swell and grow.

Before Murdio can get any closer, Lukas turns around and stares at him with his cold black eyes. "You want this halo? Come and get it!" Lukas lifts his blazing hands, causing the platform beneath his feet to lift to the ceiling. Flames explode over the structure, sections of the ground breaking off, building a stairway in the shifting terrain.

After the final piece settles, Murdio finds Lukas at the very top, staring back down at him. Lukas lifts his hand as another throne of molten fire forms behind his back. Once the final rock was in place, Lukas sits, allowing his wings to drape off the back of the throne.

Just as Murdio steps forward, flames shoot out from the pillars around the room, building a wall of fire. As the fire burns all around, Murdio looks up at Lukas sitting back in his seat.

"You don't scare me, demon," Murdio says evenly.

Lukas breaks out in a laugh and a massive roar bellows from the flames, a Fallen manifestation appearing.

Murdio's eyes widen when the light reveals the creature to be Lian.

Lukas meanwhile sits up with a grin on his face. "Destroy him, and I shall give you what I promised, plus anything your dark heart desires."

"For my demon lord and father," Lian says, bowing in the shadows of Lukas's throne.

"Take some assistance," Lukas says, smoke to rising from beneath the edges of his throne when his eyes glow brightly. Before their eyes, a single ball of fire spins into view just above Lukas's hand. Lukas then shoots the fireball, striking Lian's core, merging into his skeletal frame. The fire erupts momentarily before disappearing around Lian, fusing inside his bones. Lian's eye sockets glow brightly, spurting flames as he turns to Murdio.

"What have you done?" Murdio says, holding his staff defensively.

Silently, Lukas sits back down as smoke continues to swirl above him.

Murdio watches Lian as his entire skeleton begins to rattle and shake. Suddenly, the rattling stops as Lian's sight turns to Murdio. Before Murdio can move, Lian's skull drops off his shoulders and lands on the ground at his feet. As he continues to watch, Lian's body breaks down bone by bone to Murdio's surprise. Once the last bone breaks off, Murdio looks at Lukas, who keeps his gaze on the pile of smoldering bones.

"It's not over just yet," Lukas says when smoke begins to rise from the pile of bones.

Slowly fire shoots upward, darkening the gray smoke above the room. Then from out of the smoke, a figure appears, growing before Murdio's eyes. With its muscular limbs and dagger-like claws, it steps through the fire. Its foot crashes onto the ground and Murdio's eyes widen, watching it come closer. A demonic mix of bone and fire, the beast shakes the ground with each step. With waves of heat exploding in all directions, Murdio covers his eyes, blinking against the overpowering heat.

"What has he done to you, Lian?" Murdio asks, struggling to keep an eye on the beast.

It stops for a moment, snapping the bones in its neck, focusing on Murdio. "My name is no longer Lian; it is Demonix." Suddenly, Demonix charges toward Murdio.

Murdio spins away from the charging creature, delivering a blow with his staff across its broad back. As Demonix stumbles a step, he turns angrily, charging at Murdio again.

Once more, Murdio dodges the beast, preparing another strike. However, the quaking steps cease when Demonix stops and kicks back, hitting Murdio square in the back. Murdio stumbles toward the fire, successfully stopping just short of it. Murdio wipes the sweat from his forehead, turning around to face Demonix.

"You sure you still want the halo?" Lukas taunts from his throne.

Without an answer, Murdio charges the snarling beast, twirling the staff. Striking Demonix, he watches him fall to his knees as he lifts the staff above his head. Just as he attempts to deliver another blow, Demonix raises his massive arm, catching it and all its force. Stopping instantly, Demonix's arm trembles before falling out of its molten socket.

Unleashing an ungodly roar, the limb melts through the ground as Demonix sneers at Lukas. Demonix unleashes a great cry when another arm erupts from his disgusting body.

"I shall defeat this monster, and then I will come for the halo," Murdio says, looking at the freshly-formed arm.

Before Murdio can attack, Demonix charges at one of the pillars holding up the wall. He grabs hold, ripping it from the foundation, lifting it as shards of stone fall to the ground. Demonix turns around, sending it flying through the air toward Murdio. Smashing just shy of Murdio, it ricochets into him, catching him off guard.

The impact sends Murdio into another post next to the remaining flames. Struggling to catch his breath, Murdio blurrily watches Demonix jump over the last hurdle between them. Murdio musters his strength and pushes himself off the ground.

"This is for getting in my way," Demonix says, grabbing Murdio around the neck, causing him to go limp. With ease, Demonix tosses Murdio across the room.

Murdio struggles to push himself up from the ground, bloody saliva dripping to the ground. "Are you going to let this thing claim the honor of killing me, Lukas?"

Demonix chuckles, walking forward, once again grabbing Murdio's neck. He looks over to the surging flames as Murdio attempts to pry off its claws. "I'm going to suffocate your spirit with hatred from deep within my skeleton," he rumbles.

Approaching the fire, Demonix stops as Murdio flails in an attempt to get free. Demonix laughs loudly, holding Murdio inches from the embers. Just as Demonix tries to shove Murdio into them, his arm becomes solid rock, making it immobile. His hand then opens, dropping Murdio to the ground out of the fire's reach. Demonix roars in frustration and pain, the fire beginning to escape from his body.

"Now it's my turn," Lukas says, landing next to the solidifying body of Demonix.

"What have you done to me?" Demonix roars in exhaustion, placing his massive arms upon his cracking skull.

"You have served your purpose," Lukas says.

"I won't let you do this," Demonix says, swinging a skeletal arm at Lukas.

With ease, Lukas grabs hold of Lian's arm as the fire escapes back into Lukas's body. Struggling to get free, Lukas laughs when he rips the arm straight out. "Now you look exactly as you did before I gave you power." Lukas then tosses it into the air and over the walls of the room.

As Lukas turns to watch Murdio struggle to stand, Lian swings his remaining arm, striking Lukas in his back causing him to step forward. "That was for my arm."

Lukas scowls angrily, turning to Lian, who starts to back away. "Consider this my repayment." Lukas's body melts away between the cracks of the stones in the ground.

While Murdio and Lian look around, a flash shoots up from behind Lian. Before Lian can turn, Lukas charges through in a fiery explosion. From out of the fire, Lukas steps onto the stones, skeletal fragments showering around him. "Now, it's just you and me."

"You shall pay for that," Murdio replies.

"It's just too bad that your defeat will be both quick and painful," replies Lukas as flames leak from out of the pores in his bones.

"Maybe that is suitable for your own demise," Murdio says as his eyes glow a bright white along with his staff.

The two stand still as the wall of fire goes out suddenly, the pillars crashing to the ground. While the waves of ash burst upward, the two lock onto each other even as the wind silences the vibrations. Before Murdio can charge, Lukas uses his hands to create a rift from the open air. Murdio throws his staff as Lukas attempts to jump inside of the opening. Just before it can hit the fire, the rift disappears taking all traces of Lukas away with it.

In disbelief, Murdio runs forward, sliding to grab the staff off the ground. On guard, Murdio vigilantly looks around for any trace of the rift's reappearance. "Come out, you coward! Show yourself."

The rift suddenly reappears behind Murdio. Before he can turn around, Lukas jumps out and grabs Murdio, lifting him above the roof. Lukas then slams Murdio onto the rocky rooftop, landing easily next to him. As Murdio grimaces in pain, Lukas grabs Murdio's arm, tossing him off and down to the ground next to the pillars on the ashy ground. Lukas then walks over to the edge, finding Murdio on his stomach face down between the broken pillars.

Lukas then hovers off the ground, smirking as he begins to fly upward into the dark sky. "You're making this too easy!"

Murdio watches him, rolling over and placing the staff onto his chest, wedging it between the two pillars.

Lukas looks up as suddenly a shower of nightmarish meteors rains down toward Murdio.

Before they can fall any further, Murdio pushes upward on his staff, lifting the two pillars. He then explodes out of the ash, launching himself into Lukas just before the meteors land. He grabs hold of Lukas, whose wings flap violently out of control, causing him to change direction. Trying to keep hold, Murdio drops as his staff returns to his hands, dislodging from the pillars.

Lukas regains control as he dives through the air to the awaiting Murdio. As his speed blazes a trail, Murdio rolls away causing Lukas to slam into the ground. Woozy, Lukas attempts to slash at Murdio's face.

Dodging the strike, Murdio swings and hits the glowing halo right off his head. The halo spins off before returning to its previous golden state just as it hits the ground.

"What have you done to me?" Lukas yells, staring at his spasming muscles.

"You are not as strong as you thought you were," Murdio replies, catching sight of the glimmering halo. Out of Murdio's sight, another meteor manifests in the sky before falling to the ground. Before Murdio can move towards the halo, a meteor strikes, sending an evil shockwave in all directions. Sitting innocently, the halo flies away from the blast and back into Lukas's hands.

Lukas then places it back, allowing his body to solidify. While Lukas finishes forming, Murdio turns and dashes over to a single pillar in the distance. Lukas spots him, sending a tidal wave of flames into the ground. Just as the wave crashes into the ground, Murdio hides behind the pillar.

"Hide all you want for you are delaying the inevitable!" Lukas then unleashes two more waves upon the pillar, shaking it to its roots.

While Murdio squeezes himself out of harm, he looks upward to the flat top. Grasping the grooves of the sides, Murdio climbs his way upward, until he reaches the top of the post. Once there, Murdio pokes his head to see the hovering demon remaining in the air.

"If I remove that halo like before, then I can defeat him," Murdio whispers to himself.

He suddenly jumps off while holding the staff into the dark sky. Before Lukas can shift his attention, Murdio drives the staff into his back between Lukas's wings. Murdio finds the blazing halo above him as Lukas struggles to fight off the pain. After reaching out for it, Murdio takes hold of the halo before ripping it out of Lukas's aura. Halo in hand, Murdio watches Lukas lift himself, his hands reaching desperately above his head.

"That halo belongs to me!" Lukas screams in horror.

"You are right, and now I will release you from your sins," says Murdio as he runs at Lukas.

In one hand, the gleaming staff hangs in the air, the brightly shining halo in his other. Before he can take a swing, Lukas grabs hold of random bones protecting himself from Murdio's strike. Lukas struggles to continue a defense when Murdio throws the halo, hitting Lukas across the face.

In this moment of weakness, Murdio trips Lukas before slamming the staff down onto Lukas's ribcage. Before Murdio can strike again, a blaze appears, swirling inward. Once fully around them, the ground drops away revealing darkness. Just as Murdio shifts his sight, he drops down into the hole, leaving only his head free from the grains of black ash.

With a chuckle, Lukas jumps to his feet as Murdio struggles to break free from his ashy prison. Just as Lukas attempts to attack, Murdio's hands erupt from the ground, sending Lukas flying into one of the fallen pillars. As Lukas struggles to get to his feet, Murdio climbs back up on the stable ground. After reaching back for the Halo and staff, Murdio turns to Lukas, watching bones form in each of his hands. Murdio throws the staff at Lukas, forcing it between ribs and into the crumbling pillar behind him. Murdio stops while Lukas looks down, placing his hands onto his intact bones.

"You fool, you missed me," Lukas says, shifting back before pointing out the staff.

"Then come against me, demon," Murdio replies, watching Lukas angrily lift the bones into the air.

Lukas attempts to spring forward only to find himself unable to move. Lukas then looks back, seeing the end of the staff still within his vertebrae. Lukas tries to shake himself free when he feels the staff shrinking. Looking back to Murdio, Lukas realizes he is merely going backward. "You can never defeat me."

Murdio turns toward him, placing the halo in front of his chest. Lukas watches as suddenly Murdio's eyes glow as a pair of wings unfold behind him. "Forgive him, Father, for this demon knows not he has done." In reaction, the halo starts to pulse brighter than ever before. With a single pull, Murdio stretches the halo creating bolts of light firing from all sides.

"I will never repent!" Lukas screams.

"Amen, demon," Murdio says, watching the halo lift from his hands and hurl toward Lukas.

Attempting to get free, Lukas helplessly watches the halo spinning toward him. In a last, desperate attempt, Lukas draws a breath, exhaling an inferno, only to see it absorbed by the blinding light within the halo. Just as Lukas screams, the halo crashes through his ribcage, exploding into the pillar, disintegrating it as the trail squeezes from Lukas's bones.

As the staff reshapes inside his hand, Murdio watches as Lukas's bones flake away into the twisting wind.

"This is impossible!" Lukas screams. Lukas then looks down to watch larger chunks of tissue break off.

"Nothing is impossible with faith," Murdio says, watching as the darkness above slips away into light.

"Impossible!" Lukas roars. Lifting his foot from the ground, Lukas attempts to charge at Murdio only to disintegrate into ash.

As he watches the wind sweep away the remains, a warmth fills Murdio's body. Murdio lifts his eyes, finding the glowing halo firmly above him. He turns his head as the land around him shakes, a single beam of light dropping from the sky, landing a few feet from him. As it starts to pulse into the ground under his feet, Murdio steps forward when it starts to crack the dark facade. Murdio blinks as a figure steps out with staff in hand.

CHAPTER NINE
Return to Zithon

"FATHER, YOU HAVE COME to me," Murdio exclaims, dropping to a knee. He looks up as the light fades, seeing God approaching him.

God stops in front of Murdio, placing His pale fingers upon Murdio's bloody shoulder. He then puts His hand back to His side, allowing Murdio back to his feet.

As Murdio looks on, the wounds from his battle heal, revealing a new layer of skin.

"Indeed, I have," God says, watching Murdio stretch out his arms as the final bits of blood fade away.

"You are truly my savior," Murdio says, turning his attention to the staff remaining at his side. Murdio lifts up the staff and extends it toward God.

"Thank you," God says, waving his hand causing the staff to disappear.

Murdio then watches as two shadows step out from the light, each holding a side of a box floating between them. Catching his attention, Murdio takes a couple steps forward as the two continue to bring it towards him. "What do they have?" he asked slowly.

God says nothing, and Murdio watches as one of them places it down upon the shifting sand before making their way around it. The angel then lifts the lid, allowing the glow inside to escape.

"An old friend of yours," God replies.

Murdio opens his palm, causing the sword to lift from the box and land safely on his own. "My blade," he says softly.

"Indeed, it is," God replies, watching the two angels step back into the light and disappear.

"I just have one question," Murdio says, looking down at the shining sword.

"Ask away," God says, turning to the beam of light.

"Why give this to me now?" Murdio asks.

"Battles still remain ahead of you," God says, starting to make His way over to the cascading light.

"Shall I follow you?" Murdio asks.

God stops just shy of the light, looking over His shoulder as Murdio remains still with his sword hanging downward. "You shall return to Heaven," God replies, motioning Murdio forward.

Murdio nods, beginning to walk toward the light when he watches God step into it.

Murdio approaches, following the light from the cracking sky, down to the ashy ground. After one last breath, his eyes shut, feeling the warmth passing over his face. Once the heat passes the back of his head, Murdio reopens his eyes finding the swirling vortex of light surrounding him.

Murdio then makes his way to the edge, watching as sections of the darkness crash into the ground. He then looks downward to find himself making his toward the sky and away from the demonic destruction. Shifting his gaze upward, Murdio watches as the darkness fades away and tranquility takes over. All around, light fills everything even as clouds pass through the vortex around Murdio. Once through the clouds, a blinding light forces Murdio to shut his eyes until it passes. Once all is dim, Murdio reopens his way to find himself back on the pristine grounds of Heaven.

Murdio reaches his hand above his head, wrapping his fingers around the halo floating above. After lowering his hands, Murdio turns to watch God walk away from him. "What did you mean by battles ahead?"

"We have gotten word from some guardian angels that another Fallen lord has come about," replies God, pausing his steps.

"Can they not dispatch it?" Murdio asks, placing his wings gently over his shoulders.

"They cannot," God says.

"Why is that?" Murdio asks.

Before God can answer, Annabelle appears from the light of the sun with her bow hanging to her side. "They are no longer with us," Annabelle says, comfortably making her way over. She then places her bow across her golden armor when God turns to Murdio.

God nods before continuing toward the doorway in front of Him.

Murdio looks at Annabelle to see her staring down at her feet. He then turns to God. Without a word, God disappears silently, leaving everyone outside.

"Who is this new lord?" Murdio asks, shifting his blade in the air.

"The Faceless one from your past," Annabelle says.

Murdio's head jerks over to her, thoughts of the battle to flood through his brain.

Dropping into darkness, flames swirl around him even as screams echo about. Suddenly, a shadow rises from all around before revealing themselves. Faceless skulls staring at him, unable to reach for his blade. Then from the burning trees, Murdio turns just as flames erupt out, cutting the plain in half. Before the smoke can fade, the demon steps through, causing Murdio to retreat a step. Into the light, the figure shows his face, revealing one similar to Murdio. Skin gray as ash and a smell of death suffocating his passageways send Murdio choking back to reality.

Pale and shaky, Annabelle runs up to his side, placing her soft fingers around his sweaty arm. "What is the creature's name?" Murdio asks, seeing flashbacks of the face staring back at him

"Lazarin," a bellowing voice says. Annabelle and Murdio look around before watching God step out of the darkness. He motions for them to join Him.

Once inside, Annabelle and Murdio notice the throne in the center of the floor. Next to it, the image of Serpeda spins, revealing the its pure form hiding behind the demonic forces.

God makes his way from the side, heading over to the image. He smirks and grabs hold of the planet, staring as it continues to spin in his hand.

"Is that … ?" asks Murdio.

"Indeed, the Lost Souls are free once again," God says, staring at the image.

Murdio nods when suddenly God drops the image, watching it fall back to the ground. Just as it gets to the floor, they watch it sink through and return to its place among the others. Once in place, the universes resume their orbit around the throne.

"Who is this Lazarin?" Murdio asks, stepping ahead of Annabelle. With each step, a footprint fades from the ground behind them.

Standing by the door, Annabelle posts herself against the wall, placing her bow up against the side of her armor. Murdio watches God sit upon his throne before turning His gaze to him.

"Lazarin is an enemy made from your very marrow," God says, looking down to Murdio's side.

Murdio looks down, lifting up his armor to reveal an area of skin sinking out of place. He then turns to God who nods his head while remaining on his throne. "How can this be?"

"See for yourself," God says.

Murdio and Annabelle watch Him make His way toward an opening in the side of the room. Before their eyes, God looks at the stone wall, lifting His golden staff. As the staff glows, God raises it closer to the wall which begins to rumble. Before their eyes, the staff shrinks until it completely disappears. God stares at His hand, opening it back up to reveal a book inside.

Murdio makes his way over when God tosses it into the air. It flips end over end until it lands flat into Murdio's awaiting arms. "What is this?"

"The Final Chapter of Lazarin the Angel," God says with sorrow in his voice.

"The angel?" Murdio says. He then looks at the empty cover when golden writing appears before his eyes.

Revealing the words Lazarin Anali, God approaches Murdio. "He is the reason we kept you in the mausoleum." God watches as Murdio lifts his head quickly, frowning at Him.

"He helped us win so many battles," Annabelle says, raising her bow above her head.

"He is no longer with us though," God says, drawing Murdio's gaze back to Him.

"What do you mean?" asks Murdio.

"Lazarin, the angel, is gone and Lazarin the demon lord is here," God says.

"So, what will this show me?" Murdio asks, lifting the book in the air.

"It will show you the last days of his life story," God says, pushing the book closer to Murdio.

Murdio brings the book closer, staring at the book's cover.

"I want you to see the demon you are up against," God says, placing His hand on Murdio's shoulder.

Murdio keeps his eyes on the book while God moves His hand over to the edge of it. As they watch, Murdio opens the cover revealing the first page, finding it empty. Murdio then looks at God, staring in surprise at the empty page before him. Murdio flips the page, finding another blank page and then another. Murdio continues to shuffle through, seeing nothing but empty pages. "What is going on here?"

God then steps to his side, placing His hand on Murdio's hand. "Let me show you."

God then grabs Murdio's hand, putting it on the blank page. Suddenly, a golden chain rises from the page and around his hand. Once secure, the energy flows up his arm into his tightening chest. Before long, the energy passes through his neck into his face, causing his eyes to tremble. Beginning to water, the color of his irises fades to white, leaving nothing but a slim outline. Causing his eyes to swell, the pressure forces Murdio's eyes shut. Unable to open them, the darkness behind his lids reveal a sparkle of light from inside. Spreading all over, the pressure fades allowing him to reopen his eyes.

Around him, Murdio finds the landscape different than before, with a smell of seawater entering his nostrils. Broken buildings fill the horizon, separating the various channels of water. Debris everywhere of broken skeletons sends a chill down Murdio's spine. Spotting an opening within the ground, Murdio drops through, landing in a puddle on a wooden floor. In front of him, two angels stand at each end of the walkway. The one in front is a shadowy figure, still as stone with large white wings. Meanwhile, the other is a young angel, trying to keep his wings hidden beneath a transparent layer of skin. Struggling to take in what he is seeing, another figure appears to Murdio's side. "What is this?"

"This is my last personal message for him while he was here," God replies. God makes His way toward the figure remaining frozen in time.

Murdio steps closer to examine the being's face. "Is this Lazarin?"

"It is," God answers, staring upon the frozen expression. God then turns to Murdio, watching him begin to rise from the ground.

Once high enough, Murdio heads to the standing figure. Unable to stop, Murdio shuts his eyes just before he reaches it. Murdio's eyes re-open, finding another spirit standing in front of him. "Are you Lazarin?" Murdio watches the spirit nod before turning his attention to the vast space all around. "Where are we?"

"The moment God delivers Lazarin his message," the spirit replies. It then reaches out for Murdio, making contact with his arm.

"So why are you in here?" asks Murdio, turning momentarily from the open eyes.

"I am the storyteller, so no meaning is lost in the following events," the spirit says, turning his own attention back to the clearing vision.

Murdio watches as a set of eyes open to reveal a dark room with another figure in front of them. A hood covering its head, the figure keeps its eyes turned to the floor, allowing its wings spreading into the chamber.

"Now, Lazarin, I have come to deliver this to you," the figure says. Awaiting further, Murdio listens intently as his eyes remain upon the figure.

"Your faith and belief in humanity shall direct your future," it said before exploding into streams of light. As the particles floated into the night sky, the roof folded back onto the walls just as the last particle left the room.

CHAPTER TEN
Lazarin's Vision

THE FLOOR WAS EMPTY as I wiped my eyes and looked over the edge of my bed. Sitting on my legs, I tried to figure out if the whole thing was a dream. I mean, come on, how does a twelve-year-old brain digest the fact that God himself came down to talk?

I then took a deep breath as I laid my feet onto the marble floor unsure of the consequences that would ensue. As I took my first step toward the door, I reached out and grabbed the doorknob. When it opened, I found a bright light and a new sense of curiosity. I then stepped into the light with the hopes that I would be safe wherever it left me.

As the light faded, I found myself inside a bathroom before a dirty mirror. I looked around as I tried to figure out where I was as my gazed switched to my wrinkled hands. My eyes widened as I quickly wiped the grime from the mirror, which revealed my current appearance.

Suddenly, a snarl echoed, and I struck the mirror with my fist breaking the glass. As I looked around the room, my hand dripping blood, my eyes located a dirty curtain. I walked over and pulled it back which revealed the city's skyline.

As I stepped closer, I grasped hold of the sides and peeked downwards to the street below. The street was crammed with cars of all colors, yet nothing moved below. I looked up to find a massive wave as it approached the coast when it began to crash through the streets. I rushed inside as the water engulfed the streets with every turn. As the water reached my building, I remember I turned in horror as the water rushed inside.

Before the water washed me away, I jumped onto a sofa up against the wall. I watched as the water continue until it broke a window which allowed it to fall off the other side. Left with only puddles, I found myself in the silence of the building. I then regained my breath as I walked back toward the hole that allowed the water inside. I looked back out in an attempt to see the city's destruction. However, to my astonishment, all I could see was the water which stood stagnant over the road. All was calm, except for the gentle waves on the water.

As I looked on, buildings in the distance began to topple over. I then looked up at the clear sky. It was as if God had tried to cleanse a new future from the current state. I let out a deep breath and returned my attention to the waterlogged room behind me. As I stepped through the halls of puddles, I struggled to comprehend my next step.

I mean, really, if I get out then what do I do?

I approached the elevator doors which sat next to the stairway. Just as the despair and sadness set in, a crash from the floor above which caused me to step inside the stairwell. Once there, I found the same emptiness that had filled the last floor.

"What the hell is going on here?" As I yelled to the heavens, another sound echoed through the different cubicles.

"Help!" a voice cried.

I looked all over for the source but found nothing until I approached the elevator door. I walked up and leaned against it as I tried to hear anything. As my ear pressed against the cold metal, I crashed through it onto the puddle-covered floor, brutish sounds coming from the other side. I picked myself up and walked over to the floor just as the noises became a chorus of cries.

"Please let there be someone out there," the voice let out.

"There is, but I have no clue how to get you out of there," I replied. I looked around in search for something to help.

As I hurried through the corridors of offices, a window at the end of the hall exploded. I continued to watch as, from out of the light, a golden box dropped onto the tile floor. It sat there on the floor with golden chains connected as it hung over the side of the building.

My nerves frayed, I made my way to see what exactly was within my grasp. I then knelt and placed my hand on the cover, water surging around me. With it enveloped in the light, I grabbed the lid and lifted it open. Light gushed out, which caused me to hide my eyes from it. When the light dimmed, a metallic spear sparkled, barely fitting in the box. I reached and lifted the spear to examine it further. As I examined it, a shadow stepped into the light beyond the opening.

"Can I help you?" I asked as I rose to my feet.

"I bet you're wondering what this is for," a voice replies as it floated toward the window.

It landed swiftly as I continued to watch, the spear remained at my side. As it stood there, it flung off its coat and extended its wings, which hung well past its body. It then shifted its gaze over to me as it extended its hands to me. Suddenly, the spear glowed before it exploded out of my hand and landed in the being's hands.

"So, what is that for?" I asked as I watched the being keep its eyes upon the spear.

"This," it replied when it raised the spear and threw it in the narrow opening between the doors.

As I watched on, the being wrapped a golden thread around its hand which tightened its hold. Now with a firm grasp, it raised its other hand over its head and dropped the cowl off its robe. From beneath, its halo appeared above its head with a glow brighter than any sun. It then grabbed the golden thread and quickly locked it around its other wrist.

"With God's fury!" Suddenly its arm jerked back which sent a pulse toward the lodged spear. The spear screeched before it rocketed back into the being's grasp.

"That's some spear," I said as I turned only to find the being had disappeared. Shocked, I looked all over and found no trace of it when I single gleam caught my eye.

I looked and found the spear flat on the floor. As its reflection shined in my eyes, I knelt down to reach for it. Once I had it in my hand, I quickly turned to the elevator's door before I looked back down at the spear. I then raised it up and threw it as hard as I could toward the hole previously made. It struck with an explosion as it pierced the metal just outside of the hole. I quickly forced my way through the debris where I found the spear inside a chunk of rock. The spear jumped back into my hand as I watched as water began to seep from with the cracks in the wall.

"That's not good," I murmured to myself.

Suddenly the doors crumbled, which released a tidal surge into the room. As it continued closer, corpses floated inside. I looked at the calm water as I examined the bodies as they laid throughout the room. As I made my way to the closest, the water level sank below my ankles.

With spear in hand, I nudged the body when it imploded as it fell beneath the undertow. As I wiped away the water from my eyes, the others followed as they sent matter through the current. I quickly lifted the spear over my shoulder and walked over to the elevator.

Before I could get there, a twined rope dropped from nowhere which landed at the bottom of the elevator shaft. I continued to watch when a figure with bluish skin slid down the rope and prepared to unleash an attack from an unrecognizable weapon. I lifted my spear quickly, using it to defend myself from the creature's blows.

The blows fizzled at the contact, the staff aglow in my hands. After the last shot had disappeared, I looked up to find no trace of the figure or the rope he slid down upon. I rushed to the elevator doorway with still no luck in my search.

"What was that thing?" I asked aloud.

"An Aquara," a voice answered.

I turned when I found myself face to face with the same being who had given me the spear. "What exactly does that mean?"

"Well, it is a being designated to this area by the mighty evil," the being said.

"What are you saying?" I asked.

The being smirked as she sensed my confusion. "Before you ask, all I can tell you is that for you to survive, you will need this spear."

Before I could respond back, a mighty gust sent me backward and then down the darkened hole. Desperate, I looked for any sign of how I could survive such a fall. Before I hit the ground, the spear threw itself into the wall which caused me to shift my direction behind it. Unable to stop, my body slammed into the solid wall to the side of the spear.

"Ouch, that hurt." After my sight returned to normal, I looked down to my feet, which swayed just above the elevator itself.

Just as I took a deep breath, the spear retracted which caused me to land on the elevator's roof. I then kneeled and opened the hatch to reveal the green interior of the elevator. Inside, I moved toward the controls and pressed the button randomly which dropped it quickly. As I struggled to brace myself, it suddenly jerked to a stop. The doors opened to reveal the first floor, completely untouched by any of the destruction outside. However, outside the room and beyond the sealed windows, water covered up the light, which allowed darkness to settle in. I slowly made my way as I stared at the tossing water outside.

"Stop right now," a voice said.

I turned to find the source when I found the end of a gun in front of a man who shook nervously. The man approached me as he kept the gun aimed straight between my eyes.

"Can I help you?" I asked.

"You can drop that spear and tell me who you are," the man answered. As I debated, the man remained still, dripping water onto the marbles tiles beneath our feet.

"My name is Lazarin, and I cannot release my hold upon the weapon," I blurted out.

Without an answer, the man angrily lifted the gun as sweat dripped from his brow. A loud bang rang out, and I clenched my eyes shut, trying to control my emotions. I reopened my eyes slowly, the man trying to reload the gun.

He then looked up at me, struggling to load the chamber. "Don't you move."

I laughed as I lifted the spear up and aimed it at him threateningly. "What do you want to do?"

"I'm sorry for that, I was scared," the man replied as he dropped his gun and sobbed. The man rose to his feet as he tried to regain his composure with his gun laid on the floor.

I then lowered the spear back towards the ground as the man wiped away the tears which remained on his face. "What happened here?" I asked the man.

Before the man could respond, a rope dropped down behind the man, drawing my attention. As I tried to get closer, the being from the elevator appeared and pulled out its weapon once more. It fired a shot that struck the man in his back which caused him to stumble forward. The man fell into my arms and his body exploded into globs of water which crashed into the ground.

My gaze switched to the being as I watched it walk toward the window. "You're trapped!"

The being grinned, which bared its jagged teeth, before it leaped back-first into the glass behind it. The window remained intact as it somehow materialized through it and jumped into the flowing currents beneath the water.

I ran toward the window and watched as it faded into the depths of the sea. After I examined the body of water, I turned around and caught sight of the rope, which swayed in the air. I walked up and extended my hand to grab hold. As my hand reached the line and pulled down, a pool of water crashed down on me. Soaked, I watched as the water somehow seeped through the floor. My attention shifted to the water which dripped from my pruned fingertips.

"Greetings, Lazarin, do you remember me?" voice echoed.

I shook off the last drop before I turned my attention to an enormous figure hidden behind a hood. "I do not remember a face hidden in the darkness."

"You must listen to what I have to say," the voice said, a staff materialized before my sight. It then slammed the edge of the staff into the ground, which sent a shockwave through the tiles. Before it could reach me, I jumped over and watched as it faded before it made it to the window.

I bowed my head, realizing I did recognize Him. "So how may I be a service to the Holy Father," I replied.

"I come with a quest that you must complete," God said.

I nodded my head as God walked toward me with staff in hand. "What do I have to do?"

"Defeat the great evil that plagues this land," God replied as He pointed to the spear.

"With this?" I replied, as I looked down at the spear.

"The evil you seek is at the center of the whirlpool," God said, mist suddenly showering down. Within the drops, a picture of the vortex came into view.

"So why can't you defeat it?" I replied as I got closer to the image.

"I cannot get involved in events that transpire on the road of destiny," God replied. As the last word left His mouth, the image zoomed into the center of the whirlpool.

Suddenly, my eyes widened as it showed an army of the Aquara with larger ones who led the charge. The massive leader stood in front with a snarl, looking like it could pierce the image with its blood red teeth. The being then roared, which sent a charge through the troops, which sent them into an uproar. The image disappeared as God turned to me, the mist evaporating.

Before I could turn, God vanished, which left me once again alone. I walked around the room with a spear in hand as I looked for a way out. Not long after, I made my way over to a window as I hoped for a glimpse of life. As I stared, I struggled to separate the destruction from the corals that had begun to grow around the ruins.

Cars tumbled about as schools of fish dispersed around the trees that still stood. I shook my head when I suddenly spotted a stairs sign strung from the ceiling. I hurried towards the sign when I found a door with a tiny window which revealed the stairs on the other side. I then pushed open the door and watched as water escaped and landed on my boots. As the water stopped running, I found the staircase in decent shape beyond the occasional puddle. I then proceeded up the stairs to reach the water's surface.

As I ran, I counted the doors, knowing how close I was to an exit. Just as I approached the fourth floor, the water had disappeared, the concrete to dry.

I hit the last stair and crept closer to the door with my spear held tightly. With my other hand, I reached out and twisted the door handle open. With ease, the door swung open, and I poked my head inside, finding nothing. My eyes moved around as I made my way inside the hallway which led into the corridors of offices.

"It's like nothing happened on this floor," I breathed.

Not even a chair out of place, I made my way toward the wall of windows which revealed a newly minted night sky. The moon fresh from hiding, I made a turn past one of the office barriers when I found something unimaginable at the time. There next to the window stood a beautiful woman with flowing hair down her back.

"Are you okay?" I called quickly.

The women's head turned quickly as I failed to consider that this could be a mirage. "Are you a water demon?" the woman asked to my relief.

Before I responded, I noticed a cut on her arm which had left trails of blood up and down her pale skin. She looked down and wiped off the blood with her hand which left a red stain. She scowled in disgust at the drying blood when she placed her hand up against the wall nearby. Her hand drifted down, leaving a smeared print in its wake.

"I am merely a human," I replied.

Without a word, she shifted her sight out to the peaceful world just beyond the glass window. "My name is Alice, and I have seen horrible things outside this very window."

"Nice to meet you, I am Lazarin," I replied.

"What are you doing here?" Alice asked.

"Trying to find a way out there," I replied when I pointed toward the window.

"Why would you want to do something like that?" Alice asked.

"I need to defeat the evil outside these walls," I replied. I watched Alice's eyes sour as she thought about what I said.

"Those things destroyed my family," Alice replied. Her hands shut into fists as the memories began to replay, her eyes watering.

I just stood there and watched her cry softly as she remained silent about what she was seeing. As the silence began to overtake us, something knocked violently against the door. Our eyes widened as we turned our heads to the door behind us, which began to rattle. The door exploded off its hinges as a gush of water swept us off our feet and into the roof. The force sent us into the tiles and entangled us with the wiring hidden there, the water receding and leaving us trapped.

As I tried to break free, I looked over at Alice, who attempted to squirm free, too. Blood dripped down her forehead and off her chin as she continued to struggle. My hand twitched when I realized that the spear was still in my grasp. I closed my eyes and jabbed it upward, piercing the ceiling. I reopened my eyes to find how narrowly it had missed my body. Then with all my strength, I dragged the spear through the bracket between the wall and the ceiling.

It slowly ripped it from its screws when I stopped my attempt for freedom. Just before I looked over, Alice looked at me with tears in her eyes when she slipped from the tangled wires. I then quickly looked upward and continued my work when the bracket popped off. As it fell away, I dropped along with it onto the drying carpeting beneath me. Once I landed with a thud, I looked over to Alice only to see her flat on her back as blood covered her face. I stumbled to my feet and rushed to her side as she lifted her hand up to touch her new wound.

"What happened?" she asked as she tried to sit up.

"One minute you were stuck, and the next you dropped," I replied as I wiped the blood away.

"How did you get free?" she asked as she looked at the entangled wires around my wrist.

"I used this," I replied as I revealed the spear. Its metallic sparkle had remained despite the falling dust from the ceiling.

"Where did you get that?" she said as she managed to pull herself to a chair that sat against a wall.

"You're not going to believe this, but God gave it to me," I replied.

Taking a seat, I watched her hands as they rose to her face when she began to wipe her eyes. "That might explain that," she said, pointing.

I turned, surprised to see an angel once again behind me with a cowl over its face.

"You must start understanding the power of that spear," the angel said before it exploded into a ball of light.

I turned back to Alice, the color slowly returning to her skin even though her eyes remained wide.

"Honestly, I'm kind of used to that," I replied.

"Are you ok?" asked Alice as she lifted herself from the chair.

"Yeah, I'm fine just trying to figure out my purpose," I replied as I shifted my attention back to the spear.

"Ok, well, when you're ready to confront the enemy there is something you ought to see," she said when she pointed out the window.

I hurried over and looked out to find a squad of Aquarans on top of the cars along the surface. They began to jump car to car before they grouped up down the block as we watched from the window. Suddenly, the group paused on top of a drifting truck and then dropped out of our view. "Where did they go?".

"No idea but I intend to find out," I replied. I then backed away from the window and aimed the spear in its direction.

"I'm getting out of the way," she said as she backed away. Once she was a safe distance away, she turned as I stood there with the spear in front of me.

Before I thought better of it, I had thrown the spear into the window which caused shards of glass to splash into the wet surface. The spear dropped from view as I quickly rushed to the broken frame. As I looked, I watched the spear land upon the top of one of the cars that floated in from down the street.

I glanced over to Alice before I looked back and cleared the glass from the frame. Once it was safe, I sat on the frame and jumped between the waves. I landed in the frigid water just past the car as Alice watched on from the window above. As the initial shock faded, I quickly looked all around for the car among the turbulent waters.

That's when I saw it, just laid out on the car's roof away from the waves that crashed around it. I quickly swam over and grabbed hold of the trunk as I tried to pull myself up. Cautiously, I pulled myself up as I tried to not rock the car and send the spear into the water. As I extended my arm, a single finger managed to roll it closer. Once I grabbed hold, I exhaled as I managed to stand up on the slippery roof. I then looked up to try and see Alice as I hoped she remained an observer.

Unfortunately, I found nothing behind the windows. Before I could consider the swim back, I caught sight of the truck feet away from me.

"Hey, any help?" a voice echoed.

My eyes widened as I looked around when something splashed at my feet. Then I spotted Alice's arm as it flailed just above the water. I knelt down and grabbed hold, pulling her upward. She collapsed on the car's roof, my eyes turning back to the truck.

"I couldn't stay in there by myself," Alice said finally, having caught her breath.

"It's going to be dangerous in there," I replied.

"I have my lucky table leg," she said as she pulled out a bloody table leg from the side of her pants. As it dripped blood down her leg and onto the roof of the car, suddenly an explosion rocked a building down the street.

We watched in horror as pieces of the building fell into the water, which sent waves down the street. With each wave, the car rocked as we struggled to keep our balance. Once the final one passed, we found ourselves underneath a cloud of black smoke from where the explosion occurred.

"That was close," I said to her as a couple of cinders began to jump out of the smoke.

Suddenly, one dropped onto the car which engulfed the roof in flames. We turned our attention to the truck just a few car-lengths ahead. With spear in hand, I leaped off and landed on the bed of the truck next to us.

After both cars had stopped rocking, she jumped after me, barely missing the gate of the bed altogether. With the truck in front of us, we quickly noticed bubbles as they rose from near the front of it. I looked over to Alice and then suddenly slid down into the water. As I held my breath, I spotted Aquarans all around as they stabbed the truck with rolled up metal, one posing with the rotting driver's corpse. I could feel myself growing sick as I quickly went up to the surface for air, where I found Alice.

"What is over there?" she asked as she pointed to a golden inferno that rose from off a burning car.

"Aquarans who have no disregard for resting places," I replied. I nodded my head before once more I dropped underneath the surface.

As I watched them, back at the surface, Alice sat with her weapon clenched tightly. Before I could take off behind them, Alice suddenly jumped in, which sent a ripple towards the Aquarans. It stunned them before they spotted us as we floated near the surface. With their weapons ready, they quickly swam as we watched them cut through the flowing water.

CHAPTER ELEVEN
Restoring Balance

SUDDENLY, THE WORLD GOES silent when the vision fades to black. Murdio wipes his eyes before he looks around for any sign of the spirit next to him. After looking around, Murdio freezes when a glowing hand appears from the space and lands on his shoulder. Instantly, his eyes shut before reopening to find himself between Annabelle and God. "What happened next?"

"He was taken," replies God.

"What about Alice?" Murdio asked.

"Forgotten," God replied in sorrow.

"Wait, how do I find out who he is," Murdio asks.

"You already know that," Annabelle says.

Murdio's eyes shut, trying to remember. First, the screams of his angel brethren who were lost, which came before the unsteady environment around the building. Then, the feel of the darkness on his skin to the smell of death infecting his nostrils. Getting past that, his sight minimizes, sending him outside, revealing the skeletal frame of the place. Before he can take in much more, a lightning bolt strikes which whitens out the memory. After reopening his eyes, Murdio looks over to find them staring at him in silence.

"Do you remember?" God asks.

Murdio lowers his head, his hand drifting to the blade's handle. He then pulls it from the sheath and looks back up at him. "I do."

"Good, now we need you to take a team," God says. God then rises from His throne, causing Annabelle to stand up straight. He then lifts His hand, stilling her.

"I need to do this by myself," Murdio replies, looking to God.

God shifts his attention from Annabelle to Murdio, easing back into His throne. "You were always stubborn."

"True, but this more than a moral decision," Murdio says.

"How so?" asks Annabelle.

"This is the last verse of a chapter," Murdio says.

God sits back, watching Annabelle post herself back up against the wall. "Fine but if the unholy warriors appear then the backup will appear." God motions Annabelle closer.

Annabelle stands next to Murdio.

"I want Lazarin," Murdio says, looking over at Annabelle before looking down at the bow at her side.

"Fine by me," says Annabelle.

"Well, then my children, may blessings rain over your victory," God replies.

The two nod before turning around to face the door. Just as Annabelle and Murdio go to take another step, another angel flies into the open doorway. It lands on the strip of stones before making its way toward God.

"I have a delivery for you," says the angel looking over at Annabelle.

Annabelle curiously looks over at Murdio before turning her attention back to the angel. Before her eyes, the angel lifts its wings and pulls out a soft cloth from underneath. Once secure, the angel unravels it, unveiling the new arrows to Annabelle, whose eyes shine. She grins at them, wrapping her hands around them. She places them inside the quiver along with the others. "Thank you, these shall come in handy."

The angel bows his head and lifts off, exiting the room.

Murdio turns to Annabelle who looks over at him. "What was that?"

"Just in case I need to even the odds," Annabelle replies. Annabelle turns her attention to the golden fencing in front of them. They both then start to make their way over to the main door and the guards along the pathway.

One on each side, they kneel down as they approach the exit to the outside kingdom. Stopping in its shadow, they hover above the clouds and rise over, causing the angels beneath to look up. Continuing to stare, they land safely on the other side when they turn their attention to the cloud wall.

"Well if it isn't Murdio and Annabelle," Matiek says, waving his hand.

"Hey there Matiek, how are the clouds today?" Murdio says.

"Peaceful," Matiek answers.

"Well, I need you to open it up to some chaos," Murdio says.

Matiek's grin drops when he turns around to the moving cloud surface. Continuing to fluctuate, Matiek takes a deep breath before taking a step over to the side. He then extends his hands into the clouds before pulling them back out. Matiek's fingers come out bearing two halos shining as white as the clouds themselves. He then turns back around to them before retaking the step toward the clouds. His chest swells up and then shrinks when he twists his wrists into the clouds. Then from out nowhere, the area around his hands begin to glow brighter than the rest.

Suddenly, Matiek spreads his hands, ripping a hole within the surface. Spreading wider, it starts to darken as the seconds pass. Matiek stops his hands from moving farther when he turns back to Murdio and Annabelle. "Are you ready?"

Annabelle looks over at Murdio who nods before turning back to Matiek. "Guess so."

Matiek shrugs before turning back to the thundering space in the clouds. The darkness shading his face, Matiek reaches inward and throws out his arms. It explodes into a giant opening, revealing the mausoleum that plagues Murdio's thoughts. The weather remains calm allowing the darkness to suffocate everything, only allowing the outlines of the building to be shown.

Matiek steps off to the side rather quickly. The two look on in front of the opening before turning to Matiek who peeks his head over the lip of the cloud frame.

"What is wrong?" Murdio asks.

Matiek moves his head back before looking back at him. "Don't you remember what happened last time you were face to face with this?"

Before Murdio can answer, flashes of the memory take over before his eyes. Instead of seeing Annabelle behind him, the three angels emerge from thin air with their hands upon their weapons. Their hands shake when suddenly a scream breaks the silence in his ears. He then turns to watch as tentacles sway in the heavenly air.

Unable to lift his arms, he watches them stiffen when they shoot behind him. His vision follows behind when they grab the three before ripping them off the ground. Unable to fight, they retract into the image with the angels in their grasp. The angels then disappear through the gateway when Murdio shakes the thought free. His eyes shut and then re-open once again see the opening in front of him.

Murdio remains silent when he once again looks at the opening. Without an answer, Murdio makes his way over as the others watch on in silence. He then extends his wings and lifts off into it. Distorting, the image returns to normal when Annabelle makes her way closer.

Annabelle turns to Matiek before grabbing the bow in her hand. Once secure, Annabelle nods her head before stepping into the image. After she is through, it begins to bubble and ripple until Matiek makes his way over. Before it can calm, he then reaches out and grabs hold of both sides. With a secure grasp, he shuts the two ends, returning the cloud back to its tranquil state.

Back on Serpeda, the dark skies give way to a bright light which crashes down into the dirty ground. From out of the smoke, Murdio's glowing halo appears before he steps out into view. He looks up to the sky seeing no sign of another when suddenly a lone star races across the purple sky. Before long, he turns his attention to the demonic structure before him. His eyes glittering at its might, he stands momentarily in its shadow. Hearing nothing, Murdio continues forward until he approaches the two steps to the next level. With his eyes still on the doorway, he takes the two steps upwards and then makes his way inside.

Once inside, chaos erupts behind him from within the darkest regions of the night. From the different areas, shadowy demons drag themselves out allowing their purple eyes to look around. With grizzly smiles behind arms intertwining through the specks of light, they turn to one another. All together they turn for the doorway, beginning to drag themselves over to it. Just before they can fully make it a streaking light appears in the darkness. They look up just before it crashes down into the ground. The light explodes upwards before raining down causing the demons to turn their attention. Then from out of it, a halo shines through revealing a figure from its glow.

Without a word, Annabelle steps out when the last chunks burn in the ground. Her eyes dart all around, seeing the demons and her hand remains firm around her bow.

Dripping saliva, the demons unleash a scream which sends shock-waves in all directions. As the calm returns, the doorway closes shut behind them. They then begin to drag themselves towards Annabelle.

Annabelle then turns to see one of them make a charge at her. It then dives when another charges forward. Annabelle smirks when she slams her bow into the ground. The impact forces a barrier to rise from the ground. Piece by piece, the wall grew, casting light upon the haunted ground.

The diving demon's eyes widen in horror, watching the barrier rise toward the sky. Before it can stop, it crashes into it, causing searing wounds to appear on its body. It drops into a smoking mess when the other demons stop suddenly.

Annabelle then looks up at the salivating creatures, lifting the bow off of the ground.

As the next demon makes a move, Annabelle slams a fist into the barrier, shattering it from view. The demons look on at the crumbling wall of light when they begin to make their way out of the area. Before the last one can move, the barrier crumbles to the ground crushing the demon beneath. The others look back at the searing wall as it fades from sight before turning their attention to Annabelle.

Annabelle reaches for a handful of arrows when the demons begin to charge forward. Attempting to load the bow, she momentarily takes her eyes from the demons when a scream rings out. Before Annabelle can look back, a demon slams her into the open space behind her.

She lands with a roll until her wings manage to catch the ground before she can go any further. Her hand sinks into the ground, turning her attention to a couple of feathers tumbling in front of her. Her grin turns to a sneer when she sees her quiver sitting behind the line of demons. Regaining her strength, she stands up when they once again charge forward. Her hands come together as she looks up to the glowing halo above her.

Annabelle then charges forward with her wings hanging behind her back. She jumps forward, lifting off the ground and leaving the demons beneath her. Disappearing into the darkness, Annabelle then dives downward behind them before landing safely next to her quiver. Her eyes shining with the golden glow of the arrows, she reaches down and grabs hold of three of them.

Annabelle then looks to the demons, struggling to shift themselves back to her. After loading up the arrows, the tips glow when she starts to pull back on the bowstring. Her eyes focus in when suddenly her fingers release the drawback. The arrows explode from the bow and take off toward the demons. Before they can move, the shots strike causing the demons to slam back into the darkness.

From out of the depths, explosions of light pop, casting a reflection in Annabelle's eyes. Unable to enjoy the beauty, another scream rings out turning her attention. To her right, a demon lifts up from the ground, launching itself toward her. Annabelle rolls out of the way, sending it tumbling to the ground. Dragging itself from the ground, Annabelle opens her hand causing a single arrow to pull itself from the quiver.

It then twirls into her hand when she quickly places it back into the bow. Before it can make a move, Annabelle fires the arrow, which drills a hole between its fading eyes. As darkness erupts, the demon struggles to place its limbs over the opening. It then smiles when the gap closes as Annabelle herself grins evilly.

From behind the demon, the arrow turns and once again fires. Annabelle watches it pierce between the creature's eyes and cause another explosion of light. Annabelle shields her eyes, she slowly looking back at the dimming light behind her. She looks all around, finding craters of different sizes, sending plumes of smoke into the air. Once the silence settles in, Annabelle locates her quiver as it remains on the ground between two of the craters. She then makes her way over before kneeling beside it. After picking it up, she places it back between her wings before turning her attention at the shut door.

On the other side of the door, Murdio looks back before moving toward the open chamber in front of him. Stepping inside, he looks around at a setting very different than before. Murdio makes his way when suddenly a figure appears from the poorly lit side of the chamber.

Its face behind a hood, it makes its way closer to the line separating the light from the darkness. Then from out of nowhere, the being reaches back and pulls out a long, thin weapon from off his back. He then takes hold and launches it into Murdio's direction. After losing sight of it in the shadows, a tiny glimmer reveals itself, forcing Murdio to roll away.

After hearing a thud down the hall, Murdio turns his attention back to the figure, finding no trace of it. Before he can get up, suddenly something from the darkness pushes his shoulders downward. Looking back, Murdio sees the skeletal hands keeping him down when he follows them upward. The hands led to bones which connect to a skeleton attached to boney, featherless wings.

Before he can try to get free, the two winged creatures wrap their bony hands around his arms and drag him into the center of the room. Getting closer, an evil laugh echoes out from throughout the chamber. One of the demons shoves Murdio's head down when suddenly footsteps begin to make their way closer.

His eyes staring at the dusty floor, a shadow creeps into the room. After taking a couple of more steps, it stops when the guard pulls Murdio's head back causing him to look up. Before his eyes, Murdio sees a face of the spirit except its skin was pale, allowing darkness to seep all through it.

Its eyes, empty of life, hide behind glowing red corneas when it turns to the open hallway behind Murdio. It then lifts up its hand, a whis-tling sound roaring out until finally, a thud sends it back a step. Murdio watches as the weapon returns back to the figure's curling fingers.

"Lazarin, it is not too late," Murdio says.

Lazarin's face turns in a smirk when he approaches Murdio who turns his attention to him. "I'm afraid it is."

Before Murdio can speak, he watches Lazarin's eyes drop to Murdio's golden blade. Lazarin then looks over at the spear in its own hand. He then shut his eyes allowing darkness to cause the spear to misshapen and bubble. The liquefying darkness drips onto the floor at his feet, forming a blade much more horrifying.

Murdio's eyes darken as they catch a glimpse of the demonic aura flowing throughout the blade before the guard's hand shift up to his bare neck.

Lazarin then makes his way to Murdio's side. "See, my pathetic broth-er, God is a weakness."

Remaining silent, Murdio gulps when Lazarin chuckles as he kneels down next to the forming weapon. His hand tightens around the handle, his eyes staring as it makes it way over his head.

Murdio's eyes shut as the guards tighten their hold around his neck.

As the blade continues to grow larger, it stops once it arrives at the highest point. Then just as Lazarin can bring it down, two explosions ring out from the doorway. The sword hangs in mid-air, another explo-sion shaking the room down to its frame. A plume of smoke shoots into the chamber causing the guards to take their weight off Murdio. Another explosion sends the guards flying across the room, their bones shatter-ing. Murdio looks at Lazarin as he lowers the sword.

"Wrong, Belief is a strength," Murdio says, watching two figures make their way from the dissipating smoke. Murdio steps back when, from out of the darkness, steps in God and Annabelle together. The very darkness of the room gives way to a blinding light which spreads into all corners.

Lazarin steps back into the confines of the remaining evil while they continue to make their way inside.

Once the thundering footsteps cease, Murdio turns to Lazarin as he quivers in the darkness, struggling to hide from their sight.

Annabelle looks over at Murdio while God keeps his gaze on Lazarin struggling to stay of view. "Everything okay in here?"

"Leave it to angels to outnumber a demon!" Lazarin yells.

"Enough with the games," replies God.

The roof peels back revealing the sky outside when suddenly a beam of light lights up the outside world. It then lands down into the center of the room causing swirling air to spin through the chamber. The last bit of darkness disappears, revealing Lazarin's full body standing against the wall.

"Father, you have come for me," Lazarin yells. The demonic evil falls from his skin like beads of sweat when suddenly their direction shifts back inside his pores.

"You are no longer one of His Own," replies a bellowing, evil voice.

Suddenly, Lazarin drops to his knees and places his shaking hands on both sides of his head. Struggling to keep them there, Lazarin drops his sword to the ground. "He is here for me." As the others watch, Lazarin surprisingly places his hand onto the pillar to stand back up.

"No, he is not," the evil voice replies, dropping Lazarin back to the ground.

"Step into the grace and be free from the darkness," bellows God.

Lazarin's eyes open to reveal a single red eye on his left and a glowing blue one on his right. Lazarin then rises to his feet, stumbling his way toward the swirling light. Before the evil can speak, Lazarin dives through into the sanctuary of light.

Once inside, the three watch as Lazarin seizes and shakes free from a cloud of darkness lifting from his back. Reaching the top, it fails to break free when it begins to sink down to the ground. As it arrives at the surface, the darkness sinks within the grains of the stones. After the last bit dissipates, Lazarin drops to the floor, struggling to keep his eyes open. Before anyone can move, the seeping darkness returns outside the swirling light and reforms itself. Creating an entirely new entity, the shadow opens its eyes, revealing crimson red eyes.

"He was always a confliction to our battle," roars the evil being.

"What are you?" Annabelle ask, looking over at unconscious body of Lazarin.

"My name is Lazarin," the being replies.

God then watches as Lazarin's skin stabilizes when its hands open. Before their eyes, a scythe manifests in his grasp when he shuts them around the handle. "Yes, however, now he is back amongst his faithful brothers," God replies, looking over at Lazarin's motionless body.

"This is all yours," Annabelle says, turning to Murdio. Annabelle then looks at God who then treks toward the fallen angel. Once they are both within the light, Lazarin looks over when the three shoot upwards into the sky. Murdio and Lazarin follow the light upwards out of view before they turn their sight to one another.

Lazarin charges forward through the chamber before placing a foot down. Then after causing the stone to crack, the evil explodes off the ground and lifts its scythe directly overhead.

Murdio quickly reaches down and pulls his sword to block the vicious strike. As the weapons connect, the impact rattles inside their arms, forcing them to back away. Murdio then watches as the scythe changes shape once again, becoming Lazarin's first spear.

Lazarin then throws the spear at Murdio who uses his blade to deflect it. With the weapon sitting harmlessly on the ground, Murdio grabs his sword waiting for the next move. Before long, Lazarin charges forward in a rage, allowing his arms to flail in a circle to his sides.

Murdio then kneels down and grabs hold of his halo spinning above his head. He then watches Lazarin dive forward when he slices the halo in between them. The halo strikes the demon across the face causing screams and fear to release from its figure. Down on its knees, it then covers up the wound before turning back to Murdio. With the halo dripping in one hand and the blade in the other, the creatures rises to its feet. Then with one final charge, the creature jumps into the air and drops down on Murdio.

"Forgive him, Father, for this demon knows not what he does," Murdio replies, ramming his sword directly into Lazarin's chest.

As it slumps down to the ground, Murdio looks at the halo and then swings it at the demon's head. Then with a single clean swipe, Lazarin's head drops off causing his body to crash into a puddle of darkness. Motionless, the body begins to fade from sight, leaving the head to crash into the wall. Before long, the head itself splatters into thin air, leaving Murdio by himself.

Looking in both directions, Murdio takes a deep breath before reaching his halo back over his head. Once back in place, the halo locks into place allowing its energy to heal the battle scars. After the final cut is gone, Murdio drops to his knees, looking up to the sky.

"Matiek, I am ready," Murdio whispers, lifting his hands to the heavens.

Before his eyes, a trailing light shoots across the sky before landing in the room. It then surrounds Murdio who looks all around at the destruction that lays all about. Before long the room returns to normalcy, allowing Murdio to stand, allowing his wings to release. Lifting himself off the ground, Murdio heads into the open sky above leaving the darkness in his trails. Then the beam follows him upwards, returning him back up into the sanctuary of Heaven, having restored the peace back to the world as the darkness retreats from the new life beginning to grow.

Reviews are crucial to indie authors like me. If you enjoyed this book, please leave me a review! It helps me and it helps others find my book, too! Thank you!

Also, check out my other book, The Adventures of George and Reggie!